I0547793

Resurrection
Heart

Robotics Faction – Cyborg Mercenaries

WENDY LYNN CLARK

DEDICATION

To my wonderful baby Erik, whose presence in this world
has changed my life and given my dreams new meaning. I
hope you don't read this until you're much, much older.

Other books in the Robotics Faction series:

Liberation Series – Android Assassins
Liberation's Kiss
Liberation's Desire
Liberation's Vow
Liberation's Mystery

Origins Series
Liberation Origins
Liberation's Passion

Resurrection Series – Cyborg Mercenaries
Resurrection Heart
Resurrection Hope

CONTENTS

CHAPTER 1

A bare cell in the middle of an alien jungle. Heat, oppressive heat, and humidity so bad it made the walls sweat. The stench of rot and blood.

This was the definition of hell.

Logen Traeger shook the sweat off his bruised, bloodied face. It dripped into black puddles of stale water pooled on the cracked concrete.

He sat, chained to a too-small chair, in the middle of the cell.

Hired gunner of the Antiata Deterrence Corporation, he was currently stationed on a planet too dangerous for humans. His team, the Misfits, and a second mercenary group, Bad Company, had been called in on an escort mission once it became obvious their clients, biologists of the Antiata Commercial Ventures Corporation, couldn't use their science androids to evaluate the planet's potential. The androids were favored chew toys of the local dinos. Logen had been stationed here to ensure the same fate didn't befall the biologists.

They were only a few weeks from finishing the assignment when everything went to hell.

Exhaustion, and beatings, and heat bowed Logen's

head.

Rage kept him awake.

His blackened knuckles formed iron fists. A puffed cheek and split lip joined the lines of a thousand missions scarring his face.

Outside, the alien jungle hovered dangerously close. The scream of a ferocious pterodactyl fought the growl of a poisonous, six-legged snakezoid.

He barely noted them. Deadlier creatures were the ones he couldn't hear coming.

Such as the sound of footsteps outside his door.

He tensed. The manacles on his wrists clinked.

The footsteps paused outside, and then the door opened to let in the team medic.

His older brother, Daz.

Daz closed the door and rested his broad back against it. "Please confess."

"Confess what?" Logen's voice sounded rough from disuse, and he coughed and spit phlegm tinged with blood.

"Confess the truth. Or lies. I don't care. Just confess."

"It wasn't me. It was someone else. Can I go now?"

Daz stared at him.

Yeah. That's what he thought.

Logen cleared his throat. "What do you want me to say?"

"Who killed your spotter?"

Pain lanced his chest. The sensation quickly went away, deadened by the robotic controls embedded in his brain.

"I don't know," he said.

"Who else was there at the base?"

"I don't know."

"What time did it happen?"

"I don't know."

"How was she killed?"

Smart, dangerous, beautiful Talia. With a secret smile, an iron determination, and a heart-shaped ass he wanted parked next to him on every mission. Her dark, trusting eyes saw the real man, and her short, honey-amber hair teased him with desire.

They said he had killed her.

"I don't know," he repeated, cold as the rage the cybernetic stents kept sweeping away, leaving a burn like menthol in the emotion's place.

"You better know something, or you're going to end up with a court martial."

"I don't care."

Daz folded his arms. He had always figured out Logen's secrets before. Always had Logen's back. Always watched out for him, helped him out of scrapes, and patched up his stupid wounds.

But not this time.

"Tell us what actually happened, if you're innocent."

The manacles bit into his wrists. "Don't I look innocent?"

"You look like hell."

"I've felt worse."

"Shit, Logen." Daz's eyes narrowed, glittering anger. "Why don't you explain? Your stents screwed up. It's not your fault."

The dull silver of the cybernetic stents at his temples was visible even in the shadows. Only prisoners received them. They marked him a convict out on probation. A murderer who'd committed an unforgivable crime, served time in the highest security prison, and who had been released to the mercenaries again only because the stents suppressed his passions.

Or, at least, they were supposed to.

"They're not broken," he growled. "They're working fine."

"The longer you draw out this bullshit 'interrogation,' the worse it's going to be. You're already going back to prison—"

"I'm not going anywhere."

"You're going in for life."

"The real murderer's out—"

"There's no one!" Daz's shout echoed off the flat concrete walls. Frustration twisted his features. His chest rose and fell. "Confess now, and maybe they'll let you have visitors. Maybe even Talia."

They were resurrecting her right now in Medical. She was alone, weak, and isolated.

Helpless.

"Although, if she decides to drop by and chat with you after she finds out what you did, I hope they'll allow you to be armed."

Logen clenched his fists. His guts burned, ice cold, and so did his brain. That's how hard the stents were working to keep him cool. "Who's protecting Talia?"

Daz jutted his chin. "That's not your concern anymore."

"Tell me she's protected."

"Now there's your whole damned problem." Daz threw up his hands. "You're too interested in her. She's messed with your head. Women like her are bad for—"

Logen lunged.

Daz jumped out of reach. "Shit!"

The chains held Logen back, their anchors molecularly bonded to the concrete floor. He strained with all his might to break the bonds and clawed at the air.

His brother glared at him. Once, Daz had believed in Logen. No matter how stupid Logen's actions, Daz had believed in him and respected him. Now, when he was finally trying to be honorable, the last spark of respect in Daz's eyes died.

"This was your last mission before you paid out. You were about to be a free man. We both were. And then you had to go and fuck it up."

Logen fell back, gasping, into the chair.

"Why do you always have to fuck it up?" His voice broke.

Logen stared into space, avoiding what he didn't want

to see.

"She's waking up." Disgust soured Daz's tone. "The resurrection succeeded. You have anything you want to say to *her* at least?"

His resolution hardened as the cool calm flowed back into his body. "Give her my gun."

"What does a spotter need with a four-hundred-pound wrecking cannon?"

He sealed his mouth. She'd know he was sorry.

Daz swore at him. "You know what? I will give it to her. Because the first thing she's going to use it on is you."

Waking up always hit Talia square on the jaw.

One moment, she was home on her dad's roll-out couch by the beach. Crashing waves, drifting seagulls, and her little baby brother, only a few years old, clambering up on her squeaky bed and grinning at her sleepy self, filling her with warmth like a shaft of sunlight.

The next, she was in some shit hole on the edge of civilized space running for her life.

Today was worse than usual.

She gripped the bunk with one hand to fight off the disorientation; with the other, she reached under her pillow to collect her gun.

It was missing.

She came full upright, arms out, eyes blinking open.

The room spun furiously. Her stomach revolted and heaved for her throat.

"Oh, welcome b—whoa!"

A man's hands forced her down on the bed.

Panic jolted her. She gasped, fighting the man off.

Daz appeared in fuzzy triplicate over her head. "Lie still."

No. She couldn't be helpless. Talia arched her back and clawed at his face.

"Hey! Don't move, and don't do that!"

"What... did you... give me?"

"Nothing yet. You need to stay down until the vertigo wears off. Talia!"

Her muscles jellied. Her arms trembled.

Daz forced her flat on the bed. "Stay still."

Fresh panic jolted her.

She elbowed Daz in the face.

He stepped back and covered his nose. "Goddamn it, Talia. I hate it when you show up in Medical."

She bolted upright again, grabbed a penknife off the medical tray, and held it out at the spinning, fuzzy image of him. Easing off the bed backward, she put the bunk as a barrier between them.

"What's wrong with me?" she demanded.

"I think you broke my nose."

"Why am I here? What did you do?"

"I was trying to help you. Don't be so defensive."

"Then tell me what's wrong!"

"Chill. Answers are coming. Have a little faith in your team, will you?"

She yanked out her med feed line. Hot blood coursed down her spine.

An alarm wailed.

"Now you've done it," Daz said.

Footsteps approached at a run. First in the doorway was swift Navina, their logistics officer. Her curly, dark hair tangled around her mischievous, pixie-like face.

"You're awake," she said, stopping in surprise. "How are you recovering?"

"Recovering?" Talia repeated.

"I'll be fine, thanks," Daz interrupted, examining his split upper lip in the mirror. "Oh, you meant Talia? She's ready to take on the whole jungle, or rearrange my face, as you can see."

Navina snorted at him. "You should be ashamed of yourself for neglecting your hand-to-hand combat."

He flicked his fingers. "These hands are delicate

6

surgical instruments."

"Then you shouldn't have laid them anywhere near her." Navina kept a healthy distance.

Their muscular Grunt, Iren, arrived in time to hear the last comments. "Dare I ask? Did this guy actually take advantage and try to wake our deadly spotter with a pure kiss?"

"I'm about as pure as a lump of coal is white."

"Well, it's nice of you to spread out the abuse. I'm tired of watching your brother take all the punches."

"Will someone," she gasped, "tell me what the hell is going on?"

Their acting commander, Vi, moved between the team members like a blade cutting through water. Although much smaller, she wielded her gaze like a dagger.

They all straightened. Even Talia, fighting her nausea, swallowed and shifted on her flat feet. The room spun like a bad shuttle ride. She took a deep breath and forced it to make sense.

Vi turned to Talia. "You got off the bed."

"I was looking for my weapon."

She looked pointedly at the penknife clenched in Talia's hand. "And you found it?"

Talia crawled back onto the bunk. Daz reattached her med feeding line to the hole in the back of her neck. The alarm stopped.

Members of the other mercenary unit stationed with them, Bad Company, poured through the doorway, sweating and out-of-breath, weapons drawn, and suddenly the tiny hospital bay was full of hard bodies and noise. Her fellow Misfits apologized and calmed them down, thanked them for their swift response, and Iren saw them off.

"What the fuck?" Talia demanded. "Am I on suicide watch?"

Vi answered. "You've been resurrected."

Her soul plummeted.

On the one hand, she knew it. She'd been resurrected a

few times. Every time she died, she dropped down a level of pay in the mercenaries until she reached rock bottom, Hazard Zero, and thought she couldn't fall any further. Apparently she was wrong.

"What's the last thing you remember?" Vi asked.

"Stepping into the resurrection 'snapshot' unit," Talia replied woodenly, as she tried to process what it meant. How many extra decades this one had added to her tour. "When was it?"

"Three weeks ago."

"Shit."

Her team averted their eyes, quietly sympathetic for her loss.

First, it was a loss in pay. Being resurrected was fantastically expensive, and every time she did it on the company dollar, they added it to her bill. The more times she died, the longer it would take her to pay out and become a free woman again.

Second, it was a loss of all the memories she had made from three weeks ago to whenever she had died.

And some of those, she expected, had been pretty damn good.

"How did it happen?" she asked.

"We're still trying to figure that out. You were at Base Two with Logen. He came back. You didn't."

Logen.

His name, like his low and sexy voice, thrummed through her veins to pierce her suddenly thumping heart.

For the first time since entering the mercenaries, she had started to experience the sunlight feeling in her chest once more. Probably she'd experienced it a few more times in those missing weeks.

Logen was the cause.

His powerful thighs clenched like pistons, his biceps bulged at the kick-shock from the massive guns he wielded, and his frightening lethal grace saved them both from countless no-win-situations.

Although he was built like a god of vengeance, when he dared crack a smile, the sunlight streamed into the granite bunker around her shrapnel-studded heart. The day he stopped double-checking her targets and simply shot what she marked was the day she knew she had passed his test, and she had swelled with pride, because he trusted her.

It helped that his muscular body made her want to crawl onto his lap and lick him from top to bottom. Probably she hadn't given in to that forbidden temptation in the last three weeks.

Probably.

"Is he okay?" she asked.

"We're trying to work out exactly what he did to you. I'm sorry, Talia."

An ugly, slimy fear crawled out of her belly. "Wait. What are you saying?"

Vi's face said everything.

No.

Logen liked her. They had even kissed. He was different from the rest of them. He was a good man.

Her heart sank into a black sea. Talia had been wrong about a man before. Could she have been wrong again?

Her acting commander thought so. "The one who killed you is Logen."

CHAPTER 2

Three weeks earlier...

Logen folded his tall frame into a canvas chair in front of the first, and what would probably be the last, team bonfire.

They scored a night off. While Bad Company conducted the biologists down south for a nocturnal sea trawl, Iren got the bright idea that their team should have a little fun. And for some reason, Vi had smiled and here they all were.

In the middle of an alien jungle, at a gorgeous waterfall, skinny-dipping in a pool so clear a man could see all the way to the bottom.

Well, Iren was skinny-dipping. Daz was fishing down-river, Vi was meditating fully clothed under the churning power of the falls, and Navina was taking holos of herself next to the ugliest creatures he had ever seen. Now she posed with a sack-on-four-legs the biologist called a harmless "ground rooter."

Logen tended the fire, snapping dried branches in half and adding them to the flames.

Talia stood a quarter turn around the fire, in her usual

guard position. Studded with weapons, her normal utility belt looped across her generous chest, knives sticking between her squeezable breasts, she was fully capable of covering them all from any danger.

"Hey!" Iren waved at them. "Take a night off, you guys! The water's fine."

Talia glanced at Logen. "Do you want to go swimming?"

He jerked his thumb at the scars under his chest plate. "Nobody wants to see that."

She followed his gesture. Her gaze softened on his pectorals and she licked her lips.

He felt a hot pulse of longing, immediately killed by the prison-issue stents, but spicy as a memory of a warm glow all over. Being around her was like pouring a glass of top-shelf whiskey and getting intoxicated imagining the taste.

He sucked in a breath. Relaxing like this made him start to think things. Things that could never be, because of the stents, and because of his past, and because of who he was.

"Besides, this is nice," he said.

"Nice?" She squatted down, poking the fire. "I guess. I don't like the woods. Too many shadows."

"They scanned the area."

"Even so."

He wasn't walking too far from his gun either. "Better than a shit-crusted city."

"Is that where you're from?"

"Yeah. You?"

"My dad had a house on the beach."

"Sounds nice."

"It was beautiful." She drew a line in the ash. "I'm never going back."

Everyone knew she was counting the hours until she paid out. Not decades, like most mercenaries.

"Sure you will."

"No, I mean..."

He asked a question he knew he shouldn't. One that crossed a line. "You fight with your dad?"

"Not as much as I should have. I was a meek little girl."

He raised his brows.

She pointed at him without looking. "Don't laugh."

He lifted his palms in surrender. "People change."

"I met a guy at the beach house. He had a smooth tongue, a short temper, and a lot of friends. Before I knew it," she put her hand in the shape of a gun, held it to her temple, and pretended to pull the trigger, "I was waking up in my first resurrection chamber, enlisted."

Blood beat in his ears. The stents worked furiously to sweep his emotions away, fast as it kept welling.

He leaned forward. His long arms rested on his powerful knees, the standard uniform straining against his iron-hard, tensed muscles. "Give me his name and his location."

"He killed himself right after me, so it's hard to say."

"Name, then."

"He liked long walks on the beach."

"Talia..."

"It doesn't matter. It was a long time ago." She shrugged a shoulder. "I don't need anyone to fight this one for me, okay? I ever run into him again and I'll kick his ass myself."

Everyone had their story of how they had been ejected from civilian life and woken up in the mercenaries. Mostly it was accidents. Starship collisions, environmental malfunctions, biohazards. In Logen's case, stupidity.

But nowhere could he justify a kind, smart, and prepared fighter like Talia losing her life to a lowlife asshole.

"You never can know who to trust," she said.

The branch he had been intending to add to the fire splintered in his too-hard grip. The whole thing disintegrated, falling to chips between his boots.

"Anyway, you're about to pay out. Enjoy your

freedom." She rose to her feet again and swept her gaze across the glen. Her fingers curled around the shafts of well-loved blades. "Don't fuck up and land in the mercenaries again."

"It's not so bad."

"Trade you places, then."

"Okay."

She fixed on him. "You shouldn't joke around."

"I'm not."

Hope dawned in her dark eyes as she understood his offer. For a brief moment, she was the young and innocent woman who had trusted too much and lost her future to a violent asshole.

An asshole like him.

No. He crushed that thought. He was different now.

But then her hope faded and harsh reality settled like ash staining the night. "We can't switch places. You've earned it. You've been smart and lucky and smart."

She had called him smart twice.

"I have a good spotter."

Her brow lightened. "Flatterer. You double-checked my targets for years."

He was about to say something unwise about why he had done that, when Iren screamed.

They both whipped to the waterfall, but he was only pointing at Daz, who successfully carried a multi-limbed aquapede back to the campfire. With comically exaggerated fright, Iren, still naked, ran to Vi and tried to jump in her arms. She dunked him under the water and half-drowned him.

Logen's shoulders relaxed.

Talia's did at the same time, and she released her grip on the gun in her hip holster.

She shook her head, sharing his disbelief. "You'd think that guy never got off-planet before now."

He shrugged and faced the flames again. Maybe Iren had come from a restrictive planet. You never knew people's backgrounds.

Unless a person shared it. Like Talia had, just now, with him.

She trusted him. Confided in him. Not anyone else. Him.

Tingles ran up his spine.

The stents squashed them.

Daz chucked the aquapede on the fire. It sizzled and popped, and the others wandered over to watch the science experiment known as "barbecue." Open fires weren't exactly approved on an oxygen-rich spaceship, and wildlife wasn't too common in outer space, either.

Iren, wearing his pants again, claimed to have some knowledge of cooking, and flipped the carapace as it steamed.

"It's ready when its shell turns red." He handed his forked branch to Daz. "Want the honor?"

The medic set his feet and used his upper body strength to lift the steamed dinner up off the coals.

The branch snapped. The aquapede fell into the hottest part of the fire and started to smoke.

Everyone laughed and screamed and scrambled. Iren warned them it would become overcooked and inedible. The others scattered to all compass points to find something to get it out of the flames, leaving Talia and Logen again.

Iren stuck his hand into the flames, then jerked away, rubbing his palm on his leg. He turned to Logen. "I'll bet you can grab it and flip it out so fast you won't even get burned."

Well, that was unlikely.

"I'll bet you."

They watched their dinner brown, then blacken.

"I'll bet you Talia's shirt you can get it out," he said.

"Hey," she snapped.

"I'll bet her shirt you don't get burned."

"You can't bet my shirt." She crossed her arms over

her chest and glared at the already shirtless Iren. "This one's got my name on it. Bet your own damned shirt."

"Talia will kiss your burns and make them better."

"You kiss him," she said.

"He doesn't care about my kiss."

Logen studied the flames, more to shut Iren up than to give in to the bet. The aquapede was heavy. It rested on coals. He would definitely burn something.

"She'll kiss you," Iren told him again.

Talia frowned at Iren.

Logen looked at her, intending to reassure her that he wasn't going to do it. But, instead of meeting his eyes, she reddened and looked away.

His breath stuck in his throat.

The crackle of the fire grew quiet and the roar in his ears grew loud.

She tightened her elbows against her body, and muttered something like, "He doesn't care about my kiss either."

But that was lip reading, because he heard nothing.

Logen stepped forward, plunged his hand directly into the flames, gripped the charred aquapede around its central carapace, and tossed it out.

His hand turned white, then red. Pain screamed up his nerve endings, abruptly shut off by the stents. Only the pound of his heart, beating hard against his hard chest, still had sensation.

Talia and Iren stared at the aquapede in amazement.

A smile started to crack Iren's face and he raised his fists in excitement, dancing over to check his prize.

She snapped, "Dammit, Iren," and moved to Logen. "Let me see your hand."

No pleasure remained from her indecision the instant before. She looked directly into Logen's eyes and cussed him out for being a dumb-ass.

All of the hairs singed off, and blisters were starting to rise on the palm and fingers.

She delicately touched one. "Does it hurt?"

Her touch was angelic. Like air. "No."

"You toasted your nerves. Medic!"

Everyone came running back. The aquapede tasted like burnt tires, which Iren assured them was no fault of his cooking. Vi glared at the three of them and made Iren run laps. Daz treated Logen, bitching about using up supplies on stupidity.

"Iren started it," Talia said, eyes red. She was obviously tired and irritated by the whole thing.

"Iren's an idiot. Don't let idiots goad you into becoming the same."

"Might be too late," Logen said.

"You're a better man."

"I don't know about that."

"Yeah, well, don't fall into old habits just because we're having a little holiday here."

He accepted his older brother's lecture since it wasn't the first time Logen had done something stupid because someone else goaded him into it. And it wasn't the first time Daz had patched him up afterward.

"Be the better man." He finished spraying the skin regeneration cream and wrapped Logen's hand in second-skin bandages. "I'll leave the scars as a warning."

"Oh, don't be an ass," Talia snapped. "What's the point of leaving a scar?"

"Like a string on his finger. A little reminder."

"Is that an approved medical opinion?"

"What are you still doing here, Talia? Are you trading in your spotting oculars for a med pen now?"

"I care about my gunner's trigger finger, thank you very much. We're not rationing the cream."

Not like one more scar would be noticeable. He already had a shit ton from the missions when they'd had no choice but to ration. Times when he'd happily take another scar in exchange for his life.

Logen squeezed his brother's shoulder with his good

hand. "Thanks."

Daz looked at him with long-suffering concern. "Only four more weeks. We'll pay out by the time this assignment ends. Don't falter, okay?"

He nodded, promising Daz not to falter. Not to get talked into anything. Not to fuck up.

Daz eyed the silver medallions on Logen's temples. They symbolized the last terrible falter, when he had committed the unforgivable act that stripped his emotions and his ranks and forever locked him in Hazard Zero, dragging his brother down with him.

Talia took Daz's side. "Don't do something stupid in your last four weeks."

"Yeah, like go off somewhere with Talia," Iren said, as he jogged by.

She rounded on him. "What the hell's that supposed to mean?"

Iren kept jogging.

A sardonic glint entered Daz's eyes as he took up the joke. "It means..."

He trailed off and a strange expression came over his face. Whatever he was about to say, he didn't say it.

Good.

Logen had stents now. So no emotions would cloud his judgment longer than the few seconds it took for the stents to activate and remove them, leaving him clear-headed again.

His older brother packed up his medical supplies and rejoined the others at the fire.

Talia lingered beside Logen at the edge of the water. "What he said."

He accepted her scolding with a smile.

She poked his hard chest. "Seriously! Don't let Iren talk you into anything dumb now."

He caught her finger in his good hand.

She froze.

But she didn't pull away. Her chest rose and fell, rose

and fell, and her gaze fixed on their linked hands. He maneuvered to slide their fingers together, palm-to-palm. Connected.

She lifted her eyes as far as his chest. There, her embarrassment stuck. Her dark eyes unfocused and her lips parted.

Standing together, he could have stayed a hundred years. Close to her. Fingers intertwined. Wishes almost linked.

But this was as close as she got.

Logen didn't fool himself. Actually kissing a guy like him, with the evidence of his crimes on his face, was like digging up her murderous ex to forgive and forget.

He was the king of wishful thinking.

Logen squeezed her fingers and let her go.

She blinked.

"Thanks." For her concern, for her kindness, for letting him pretend. He meant it.

She rubbed her thumb across her fingertips and didn't reply.

His combat boots made the lightest sound, graceful as a cybernetic soldier was forced to be, as he left.

The others ranged around the fire, except for Iren, who was still running laps around the small grotto.

Logen checked his gun on his thigh, and the angle of the moon against the stars, time and navigation—

Talia ran up behind him.

He turned to her.

Her face burned red and she gasped for breath, despite only crossing a few short strides. Determination glowed in her eyes. That determination was one of the things he loved the most about her.

She eased up to her tip-toes and cupped the back of his neck.

He started to duck to her level. Had she spotted something only for his ears?

She reoriented his face and her lips brushed his.

The world stopped.

Her lips felt soft and sweet and so good. Her breath smelled like vanilla, sweet and spicy. The moon suspended between them, a force of gravity pulling them together. Her lips yielded to his. Her body molded to his chest, her breast pressed against him, and her fingers teased the back of his neck.

He craved a deeper taste.

The night heated to a hundred degrees. The flickers of yearning in her sweet fingers, so beautiful and so hungry, lit a match in his body. He wanted to trace her lips with his tongue, wanted to plunge into her mouth, wanted to mold her body to his, wanted to tangle his fist in her short, amber hair.

And then it was over, and she was steady on her feet again, her determination burning hot as her desire. "You don't have to stick your hands into flames, okay? Ask next time."

Her words struck his skull like a gong.

A small smile curved her sweet lips. Accomplishment joined her determination. She nodded to herself, pleased she had overcome her resistance and *done it*, and she turned and stomped back to the bonfire.

He walked more slowly.

Denial remained. Had she kissed him and told him she might do it again?

Yes.

A slow unfurling of hope took root in the long-dormant soil of his chest and lifted a bright green sprout towards her unfailing light.

His cock, silent and immobile all these many years, twitched.

Impossible.

But also undeniable. It twitched again.

And then the feelings flooded in.

For the first time since the stents went in, his emotions welled, hot and pulsing, and remained. Her sexy body swayed in front of him, and his mind filled with her. Blood pulsed in his cock, fed by her delicious scent and the memory of her softness. As the heat grew, so did the piercing throb in his chest. Talia was beautiful. So beautiful. And she had kissed him. His pulse raced, faster and faster.

He wanted to kiss those cheeks, and follow the blush down her neck to her delicate collar, and then he wanted to nibble kisses all the way down her body.

The stents did nothing to stop his feelings. It was as if they had been shut off.

He felt like a man again.

His hand ghosted over his gun, his eyes swept the woods, his nose scented for danger, and she burned bright in the center of his world. Brighter than the bonfire. Brighter than the hottest star in the spattered night sky.

He would guard her with his life until the end of time. Nothing bad would happen to her. She would pay out and get back her well-deserved freedom.

He swore it.

She was the most precious thing in the entire universe. He would guard her with his life.

CHAPTER 3

Talia knew Logen had stents. That's why her kiss all those weeks ago hadn't meant anything to him. The tall, broad, powerful gunner wasn't interested in her romantically.

Being around him filled her veins with gasoline.

He was different from all the rest. She wanted to tickle him until he smiled. She wanted to lick his forbidden skin, trace those knotted scars to his masculine center, find the bulges under his plate armor, fill her palms with his massive pectorals and taut buttocks, and rub herself on every part of him. She wanted to claim him for her own. Her body slicked with hot, pounding readiness whenever he strayed too near.

He couldn't feel anything. Her hopeless crush could never be returned.

That made him safe.

Except something had changed. His stents had malfunctioned and he had killed her.

Talia passed a fitful night in Medical. Every time she jerked awake, she had to face the truth all over again.

Now it would be an additional fifty years before she could pay out and see her brother. The one who had ended her had been the one man she would have trusted with her life.

She was a fool. A weak, stupid, helpless idiot.

Talia slept attached to a monitor that set off an all-base alarm any time her heart stopped.

That monitor, and the sentries posted outside her room, and Daz snoring loudly on the pallet next to her, kept her from crawling out of bed, storming down the hall until she found the culprit, and carving her revenge out of Logen with her penknife.

The last guy she had made the mistake of trusting had slammed her head into a counter because he didn't like the way she looked at the person who took the orders for their meal.

She thought Logen was different.

She thought *she* was different.

In the grim morning, she passed her reflexes check and asked permission to leave the sick room.

Vi rested her sinuous body against a shelf. "And go where?"

"Around."

Her serious gaze lingered, burning Talia's brain like acid. Her gaze had a sharp sort of danger, like coiled smoke, and a hard heat that matched her throaty voice and unsettled all who looked too long upon her.

"I want to check on a few things," Talia said. "Such as how I died. And whether I fought back."

"You can't interview Logen in this condition."

"I'll review the evidence."

"We already reviewed the satellite footage of your final night."

"Oh yeah?" A dense, teeming jungle was too thick to penetrate with a distant satellite. "Exactly what didn't you see?"

"We didn't see another hover bubble traveling to Base Two. The following day, well past when he should have reported in, we found Logen walking out in the jungle, alone."

The similarities chilled her. She had just told Logen about her last boyfriend. Had she given him the idea?

"We scanned all of Base Two. Your blood was found only on Logen's hands."

So, then, he hadn't killed her inside the base. He must have killed her in the jungle and cleaned up his suit, but missed his hands. "You didn't find my body? No trace?"

"We don't even know where it happened."

All the more reason for Talia to take over. "Let me talk to him."

"When you feel stronger."

"I'm strong now."

Vi licked her lips. "I know you two were close. It will be hard to see the truth."

"He's already a criminal. And have you seen his perfect kills?"

Vi studied her.

She hated it. She wasn't a woman to be pitied. She would fight.

"I'm a spotter. Let me do my job." She scooted to the edge of the bed. "I promise I'll be back by bedtime."

Her legs hung like dead weights off the edge. She tried to bend her right knee. Without the panicked adrenaline, her leg didn't twitch.

Vi smiled tiredly. "You're not going to see Logen until you can move your legs."

"I can help with that." Daz dragged in an exoskeleton. "Try this."

"Hello, medical malpractice?" Navina held the other side and dragged against him. "This piece of shit collapsed on a healthy person. No way it's holding up a resurrect."

"It'll support Talia." He yanked it free. "She's got a stick up her ass already."

"Come closer and say that," Talia said, flexing her fists.

"Do it. She should whip it out and beat you with it."

"*Thanks*, Navina."

The perky navigator tucked her dark curls behind her

ears. "I'm just saying we should be patient with the patient. What's another week?"

Daz shook his head. "In another week, we'll all be out of here and Logen will be on his way to the slammer."

Vi's eyes narrowed. "Don't let your relationship cloud your professional opinion."

He shot her a bitter gaze. "Since when do we care about being a 'professional' unit?"

Vi shut up.

"Here. Let's do this." Daz offered Talia his shoulder to help her ease into the exoskeleton.

Talia ignored him and swung out of the bed lethargically. The resurrection created her whole body in a pristine adult state, but the muscle-training programs never had long enough to rebuild her strength.

She slid out of the bed and into a heap on the floor.

Fuck.

Sweat beaded up on her brow. Her stomach churned. She gasped for breath.

Daz leaned over her. "Sure you don't need a hand?"

She hated him. She hated all of them. She hated the weakness in herself.

Daz would leave her on the floor if she didn't ask for help. Actually, that was something she liked about him. He never pitied her, and he never tried to do something for her against her will. The others had had to learn.

Well, not Logen. She never minded his help. He never made a big production of it either, just doing what needed to be done and moving on.

Out of all of the mercenaries, out of all her teammates, why was he the one?

She lifted one shaky arm to Daz.

"Up we go." He set his feet and flexed, groaning as he lifted her. She was a big-boned woman, and he had none of his brother's impressive mass. He inherited wiry strength rather than bulk.

When her feet rested on the exoskeleton soles, the calf

and thigh bands tightened, encasing her in a thick wrap around her butt, cinching her waist. It interfaced with nerves in her spine.

She straightened.

The exoskeleton tightened to her frame with a quiet whoosh.

"See? She can walk." Daz let go and stepped back. "Take a few steps."

The room wobbled. Blackness teased her vision. She lost her balance and nearly toppled.

Vi and Navina watched her, stone-faced with concern.

"On second thought, I'll get a hover disk." He left.

Talia wobbled and caught the bed to arrest her collapse.

"Okay, look." Vi stopped them with her gaze. "We're already down half the team. I'm not prolonging your outage due to idiocy. You can see Logen when you can damn well walk there."

Fury boiled in her belly. "I have the right—"

"Until then, you can review *the evidence*." Vi lifted one brow, demanding obedience. "And that will be good enough."

Fine. For the moment, it sufficed.

She fought the light-headedness. "When can I get my gun?"

"When you pass your physical and your marksmanship exam. Until then, I don't want you running around Base with a weapon."

She reached for the penknife on the bunk.

"*Any* weapon. You're going to fall over and stab a Good Samaritan. Leave the surgical implement here."

Talia lifted the penknife to the shelf over her bunk, secretly rolling it to the seam of the wall so she would have it at hand.

Daz returned with a hover disk that fastened to the back of the exoskeleton. It lifted her off the ground a few inches. She had to hold her posture stiff to keep her heels from catching on the ground. If she couldn't remain upright, Vi decreed she had to get back in bed, so she gritted her teeth, swallowed back her awful nausea, and floated after her team through the base.

It looked different than she remembered.

The halls, once jammed full of biology samples and equipment, were now lined with crates. The mess hall, once decorated with maps of swamps and the things that bit people there, now contained only a few tables and the food reprocessor. And the biologist wing of the base, once filled with noise and excitement, was now quiet with the scurry of final adjustments, species to be bagged, and furious packing.

"Spot." Mercs from Bad Company nodded to her as they passed, laden with shuttle-loads of equipment. "Hey."

She tightened her jaw and returned their nods.

"Talia!" A group of biologists converged on her. "Are you okay? Welcome back to the land of the living! Are you sure you should be standing upright?"

"Yeah," she said. "Thanks."

They faltered. "Um, well, take care of yourself. See you…."

Civilians. She wanted their freedom so bad it tasted bitter on her tongue.

Vi glanced up at her as the biologists blushed and headed away. "You could thank them gracefully. They worried about you."

"I didn't ask them to."

Vi raised her brows, but said nothing.

The officer conference room was a closet-sized hole tucked in the back corner of the base, behind the Bad Company CO's private office, and it smelled like old socks. A few screens and chairs were set up, and the ubiquitous open windows were blocked by polarizing glass. The comm to the orbiting main ship Upstairs hissed gently between updates.

She joined Chaelee, cheerful spotter for Bad Company.

Everyone quickly grew bored by the technical discussion, and left the two spotters to pore over their area of expertise.

"The interview holos are here," Chaelee said, sitting with her in front of the communications consoles.

Her unusual porcelain skin was pure white and, behind her magnification oculars, her startling gray eyes were rimmed in dark lashes and framed by darker brows.

She brought up the list of dated interviews on one main screen and handed Talia a pair of spotter's oculars. "The reconstruction based on Logen's original, undocumented testimony is here, and his declassified files are here. We've also got the satellite images, although of course those are useless."

Talia affixed the oculars to her nose so the clear lenses covered her eyes. "You've seen all these?"

"About ten times. I'm ninety percent certain you were eaten by a warm-blooded reptile."

Ugh. Some memories she was glad to have lost. "And the satellite images are useless?"

"Of course. It's a dense jungle!"

Talia immediately liked Chaelee. They hadn't had a chance to work together much because they were usually split with different groups of biologists. "That's what I thought."

"People are too reliant on satellites, when a hundred things could make them go wrong. In a jungle like this, I could pace a hover bubble back and forth between the bases and you couldn't see a thing."

The woman turned to Talia brightly. "Oh, by the way, I heard you have a little brother like me."

Talia's heart squeezed. "Who did you hear that from?"

"Iren."

Of course. The blabbermouth.

"I never got to meet mine," Chaelee said. "My mom was pregnant when I went in. How about you?"

"He was five."

"How sweet!" Chaelee clasped her hands to her chest. "I bet he was wonderful."

Talia swallowed the welling of emotion. "Yeah. He was."

"Is that why your parents couldn't afford to buy your resurrection?"

"My dad was on his two-decade paternity leave and my mom invested everything in a new business."

"I'm sorry."

Talia shrugged. Everyone had a sob story. Nobody volunteered.

"I talked my parents out of spending the money on me," Chaelee said, immediately proving her wrong. "And, considering how things turned out, it's a good thing."

Aside from her cheerfulness, Chaelee was notable for having died over three hundred times; many of those were from friendly fire. Talia had died five times now and was angry for having to pay the resurrections off. Chaelee wouldn't pay out until after the heat death of several suns.

"It shouldn't be so expensive," Talia said supportively.

"At least it's an option. I feel so bad for people who can't be resurrected. You just die. Forever. Resurrection is really a miracle of the modern age, don't you think?"

Enough.

"If I was eaten," Talia changed the subject back to the main topic, "then could it have been an accident and not anyone's fault?"

Chaelee's dark brows immediately sobered. "I wish. But three weeks ago, we were still running the force shield over Base Two. It was damn near impregnable. If something got you, either one of you let it in, or something convinced you to go out."

Such as running for her life from a homicidal partner.

"It's too bad," Chaelee continued. "You're already down several team members, right? Now you're down a Gun. If the Misfits get disbanded, you should put in a transfer to Bad Company."

"You don't need another Spot."

"You're pretty dangerous," Chaelee indicated the stylus Talia had stolen from the room and secreted in her hospital suit, "so you could probably be a Grunt."

How flattering. But she'd never had to prove herself in actual hand-to-hand combat, and had no interest in trying. "The Misfits aren't getting disbanded."

"Oh, I heard you might be. Vi's only your second, right? Where's your CO?"

"Sirus is on leave."

"For this whole assignment?"

"For the past fourteen years."

Her jaw dropped. "Are you sure he didn't desert? That's a hell of a long vacation."

Talia hugged her elbows. Once, she'd opened up to Sirus. *We all go home.* He'd said it over and over, and he was the first one to have complete faith she would pay out, despite being in Hazard Zero. He'd been the only one to see beyond her tough exterior to her inner fears, and he'd actually started her on hand-to-hand combat training, to help her get over them. If he'd stayed on, maybe she could have finally conquered her ghosts.

Maybe she wouldn't have let herself get killed by another goddamned man.

She didn't want to think about past betrayals. "Let's start."

They watched Logen's first interview holo. With her oculars pointing out all the micro expressions and hidden emotions, she struggled to focus on the landscape of the human face.

Not on the man whose undeniable presence made her heart thump, her hairs shiver, and her legs squeeze together. Even though she knew what he was, her body couldn't help itself. She'd craved a taste of him for so long.

That was probably how he drew her in.

After half an hour, Talia had to turn the holo off. "Logen doesn't say anything."

Chaelee bit her lip. "No. Not at all."

Her oculars picked out no emotion on Logen, hidden or otherwise. The whole time, the rock-hard gunner sat there, staring at the Bad Company CO, who railed and accused him and threatened violence. Then he stared at Vi, equally powerful, equally silent. And then he stared at Daz, and Iren, and even Navina.

Then the Bad Company CO returned and started interrogating with his fists.

"He says he's innocent, but he won't say what happened that night."

What the fuck, Logen?

"He never says anything that proves he knows too much, either," the eternal optimist said.

That was also true.

Talia rubbed her aching forehead.

Chaelee shrugged. "But anyway, there's nothing here. I'm sorry."

Except the key to everything. Talia removed her oculars and rose with the hover disk.

"Heading back to your room?" Chaelee asked.

"Eventually. Where's Logen?"

"I don't think I'm supposed to tell you that."

Fine. She would find him herself.

Chaelee stopped her with a grin. "Of course, I could happen to walk past where he's being held…."

She gripped her exoskeleton. "Lead the way."

Chaelee stopped by the reprocessor for coffee, chatted with her teammates, and eased Talia's way through the base. She was so friendly and engaging. Talia found herself relaxing.

Most of the mercenaries in Hazard Zero carried a hell of a lot of baggage down to the bottom with them. Being with Chaelee reminded Talia of her civilian life, and she craved spending more time with the woman. From the gathering of followers who happened to be in the same area as Chaelee, obviously she wasn't the only one who felt that way.

"I'm glad we finally got to spend time like this," Chaelee said to Talia quietly as she made their escape. "Sorry it happened under these circumstances."

"Me too."

They reached the end of the long, central hall running north and south through the base. Chaelee stopped her at the southernmost door.

She suddenly clasped Talia's hands, surprising her. "You'll have to tell me more about your little brother. Come over to my bunk when you get out of Medical. We'll trade stories."

"Sure."

Chaelee grinned like sunshine. Her touch was gentle and heartfelt. "Good luck with your gunner." She threw open the door.

Vi, Navina, and Daz stood on the other side.

"Going somewhere?" Vi asked.

Chaelee blinked rapidly as she struggled to come up with a plausible story. Vi obviously frightened her, and her white cheeks reddened. "Well. We, uh, Talia and I wanted to walk, mmm, for exercise."

Vi raised a brow.

Chaelee swallowed. "Uh... so..."

Talia cut her off. "I'm speaking to Logen."

Everyone looked at Talia.

Navina shook her head, concern on her pixie face. "You can barely stand. One look at you and he'll know you're not a real threat."

"Oh, he knows me better than that."

Talia faced the remnants of her team, gearing up for a fight.

Vi cut her off. "You're still upright. You want to see your own murderer? Let's go."

CHAPTER 4

They exited the main building and crossed the compound.

Her feet ghosted above the bare dirt. Overhead, the bluish bubble of the force shield repelled wildlife, but was porous enough to let through misty rain and falling leaves from the thick green canopy.

The main building was shaped like a half circle around the shuttle landing field. The officers' quarters stood at one tip, while the building curved around sick bay and the dorms in the middle, and reached the fragmented outbuildings at the bottom tip.

The comm tower stretched up to the trees and shaded over the whole compound.

Iren was hanging around outside one of the storage sheds, tossing a fist-sized rock up in the air and catching it. He saw them and dropped the rock. "Shit. You'll have to wait a minute."

Talia swallowed her nausea.

Iren squinted at her. "You okay? You look awful."

She nodded.

He shook his shaggy head. He was new, but already knew better than to push. "Try to get him to confess. As quickly as possible. For me, please."

A scream ripped through the building.

It jolted Talia and stuck her with pins and needles. Where the hell was her weapon? She flexed for it.

No one else reacted.

"What the hell's going on in there?" she demanded.

"The honored Base Commander is wrapping up another productive Q & A session," Iren said, irony dripping from his tensed jaw. Sweat beaded up on his forehead, matching the dampness on hers. "Oh, wait. Here he is."

Bad Company's CO shoved the door open and emerged.

Because their CO was on permanent vacation, the Misfits were always forced under the boot of any other mercenary unit. Vi was only a second, and thus she was always outranked. She had other talents that kept the boot from crushing them too hard. This was a time she had not prevailed.

Squatter and more solid than Iren, Bad Company's CO had the lamppost jaw and brow of a man not easily dissuaded—which was why it was notable how studiously he avoided the daggers thrown from Vi's deadly gaze.

He picked something white out of his knuckle and pitched it on the ground.

"Medic," he noted Daz, and held up his meaty, bloodied knuckle.

Her stomach turned.

Daz jerked a thumb over his shoulder. "Medical's that way."

The CO nodded to Talia. "Welcome back."

She muttered a reply.

He sauntered off with Daz.

Talia looked down at the white thing on the ground. It looked like a tooth.

No way.

She rounded on Vi. "Are you intending to let him beat the stents out?"

Vi set her jaw. The last person she desired a talking-to from was Talia. "Logen's going back to prison. If he cooperates, they'll stop the court martial."

"He's a member of our team. The Misfits. That used to mean something."

"Until Logen tells us something, I have no choice."

"So you're fine if he gets sent up in pieces, then."

"He killed you."

"Then why's he still here? Do you really care whether he shot me in the back or strangled me with his gun strap?"

Vi's chest rose and fell. Facing off against Talia.

"Unless there's something you're not telling me," she said. "It's hard to cooperate when your mouth is full of someone else's fist."

She leaned down and picked up the tooth. "He might not have been working alone."

What the fuck?

Heat smacked into her in a wave.

Her other teammates shifted uncomfortably. Was one of them a murderer too? Or Bad Company? Or the biologists?

It explained why she was under suicide watch. They weren't afraid she was going to kill herself. They were afraid someone else was going to do it for her.

"Anything else you forgot to mention?" Talia demanded.

"Don't tell Logen," Navina said, casting a worried glance at Vi. "We don't want him to tip off his, uh, accomplices."

Accomplices, plural. More than two people were trying to kill her. Fantastic.

Iren checked his wrist chronometer. "You'll want to get in there. The CO will be back in ten minutes."

"If no one's beaten the truth out of Logen in three weeks, I seriously doubt another 'session' is going to crack his story," Talia said.

Her words hit home.

Vi jerked her chin at Iren. "Watch out for Talia. I'm going to talk with Bad Company's CO."

"Champion." Iren cracked his knuckles. "Don't aim for *his* teeth. I heard one of them is titanium."

They watched Vi stride across the compound, purpose in her dangerous step.

Iren stretched. "Thank the fucking stars. Way to go, Talia."

"Yes, thank you, Talia."

Iren and Navina both smiled at her with relief.

Her face heated. "I didn't do anything you two couldn't have done."

"Yeah..."

"It's impossible to argue with the CO," Navina said, "and Vi felt too guilty for sending Logen off with you alone."

"Exactly," Iren said.

Well, good that someone had spoken up for common sense. But there was no reason for Vi to have felt guilty. "It's not the first time we went off on an assignment alone."

Their smiles faded. They both shared a side-eye glance. Iren doubled-down on his smile. Navina shifted and studied the ground.

"Okay, now what aren't you telling me?" Talia asked.

Iren reached out his big hand and squeezed her shoulder. "Find out what you can. Don't get too close."

Logen had so easily fooled her. Whether working alone or with a group, Talia would never forgive him.

She nodded.

He opened the door. "Go get 'em, viper."

She crossed the outer vestibule. Through a pinhole view, Logen hunched in a pool of grim light inside the inner cell, his dangerous face ridged with battle scars.

Her heart kicked. A curl of desire squeezed in her center, pulsing awareness of the powerful, virile man.

Nothing had changed despite knowing the truth. He attracted her like no one else in the universe. She sucked in a breath, striving to control her reaction.

She'd thought those scars were beautiful, once.

She'd thought he was a protector. A warrior. A hero.

She'd thought he was safe.

Fucking bastard.

She would squeeze the truth out of him and stomp on the remaining pulp.

Talia took a deep breath and grasped the door latch.

Logen expected to see the asshole CO back with a healed hand ready for round two, and he growled deep in his throat as the figure hung back in the eastern shadow.

"Come out," he said, low and furious. "Come close. Give me the chance to kill you this time."

The figure slipped out of the shadows.

It was Talia.

Relief crashed through his body like a wave, filling his eyes with moisture and choking the back of his throat. Impossible, because he was stented. But the impossible feeling built and built, wave on top of wave, until his blurred eyes couldn't see through the salty water and his whole body relaxed and gave in, blinking streaks matching the sweat dripping down his cheeks from his forehead.

She looked better. Tall and strong, fearless and determined, and with a heart the size of the entire planet. The chest that contained it was pretty nice too, with slim hips and thick, grippable thighs, and breasts that begged for his palms, and a mouth that promised wonders for a long, hot night.

His cock twitched to life.

Also impossible.

But impossible or not, his insistent erection pressed against his ripped flight suit, just like it had all those weeks ago when he had last seen her.

His stents worked perfectly until the moment Talia got too close. Not anyone else. Just Talia.

Then they stopped working and he was flooded with emotions, wrecked with them.

She was alive.

"Thanks for the warning," she said, reacting to his comment for the CO.

He barely heard her. "Are you okay?"

"Fine."

She was wearing an exoskeleton cinched around the waist, and she slid forward smoothly, on the power of a hover disk. Her normally golden face looked pale, and even her lips had turned a shade of ashen. Her hands, gripping the outside seams of the metal skeleton for comfort, shook. And her eyes watered too, but her trembling lower lip suggested it was not from relief.

"Sure?"

"Why the hell do you care?"

That sounded like her. He started to relax again. "You don't look like you should be upright."

"Yeah, well, you weren't coming to me."

He shifted. The manacles clinked. "Sorry I couldn't visit you in Medical."

"I wouldn't want you to." Bitterness tinted her words. "I have a few questions."

Logen concentrated on her. Drinking in the sight.

Once, he saw her taking off her belt, shimmying out of her suit, exposing yards of creamy skin to his gaze. Moonlight and firelight had cast blue and golden glows to her rounded breasts, her hourglass waist, and most importantly, her heart-shaped ass.

He had failed her. He swore to himself he would not do so again.

And that meant not letting slip his stents failed around her. They'd stop looking for the real murderer and send him straight up to the solar station for his court martial and quick trip to prison, leaving her unguarded and alone.

"They sent you to talk to me," he said. "I've got nothing to say. Coming here is a waste of time."

"Answer my questions and I'll leave you here to rot."

"A waste of time."

"I've got nowhere else to be."

She looked like she should be back in Medical, still recovering.

"What happened on Base Two?"

He hated to see her this way.

"Start talking, Logen."

He took a deep breath.

"Now."

And held it.

Talia gripped her exoskeleton. "What did you do to me on Base Two?"

"I didn't do anything."

"Lies," she said. "How did you kill me?"

No. The rest of them hadn't believed him. But surely Talia—

"I'll start." She crossed her arms over her chest. "We went to Base Two. We packed up some equipment. We set up our bunks. Then I never slept in mine."

"You took first watch."

"And you did what?"

"Slept."

Her eyes narrowed.

Sweat trickled down his forehead. He tried to rub it away. His manacles jerked his wrists hard and clinked.

"You're lying," she said.

"I was in my bunk," he snapped.

"Until what time?"

"My turn. For watch."

Only he'd had no one to watch. She'd never come back. That's when he got up and started looking for her.

"You were in your bunk the whole time I was on watch?"

Shit. He was confessing.

Logen gritted his teeth.

"Did you black out? Did you hear something?"

He hadn't blacked out. He had been wide awake, waiting for her to come back.

They'd had a pretty heated conversation. No way could he fall asleep. He'd wanted to run out into the jungle and wrestle dinozoids. His skin had been jumping. He'd wanted to pound his fists into walls. She'd killed all his hope that night.

Then she hadn't come back from watch, and he realized those feelings were the tip of how very bad things could be.

"Did you get up and turn off the force shield?" she asked.

The force shield had been on when he got up to look for her. Hadn't it?

"Did you sneak up on me? Or did I see you coming? When did you decide to kill me? Why did you do it?"

Her questions pounded straight into his gut. Denial twisted it into a tight knot. She had to believe in him. She had to—

"How did you do it?"

The knot looped around his heart and tightened.

Everyone else thought he was a murderer. But Talia had been different. Once, he'd been respected in her eyes. She had seen past the stents. Seen beyond his past. Seen the man he could be.

"How?" she repeated.

He shrugged, not trusting his voice. Did it matter what he said? She'd already made up her mind. Just like the rest of them.

Just like all of them.

She floated closer. "Why the hell won't you say anything?"

"Like what?" He jerked against the chair. Rocking back and forth, helpless, chained to the concrete. "What's left to say?"

Furious tears glimmered in her eyes and thickened her voice. "I thought you were different."

"I thought *you* were!"

"Is that why you killed me? Because you figured out the truth?" She pressed her palm over her chest, her other palm on top of it. She took a deep breath, staring at the ceiling until the tide of tears receded, and then she glared at him with her entire force of will. "I'm an ordinary, easy to kill, undefended little girl."

He snorted.

Her lips curled. "That's what you thought."

No fucking way.

"That's what you thought! That I'd be easy to kill!"

"Talia!" He shook his head at her. "You're the single most hardest ass I've ever run into. You're constantly armed to the teeth."

Her hands clenched and released. Weaponless.

"You're a danger barehanded," he emphasized. "I'd rather face the entire rest of the team than go head-to-head with you."

She straightened and swallowed. "So you're saying I didn't curl up in a ball and plead for my life."

"Whatever happened, I'm sure you went down fighting."

"*Whatever happened?*"

"Yeah, whatever happened."

"So, what, did you knock me out and throw me outside the force shield?" she demanded.

Never mind. She couldn't hear the truth any more than the rest of them could.

"Say something."

"What does it matter what I say?" he said.

"Do you not like me? I mean, the instant your stents glitch out, you snap and murder me. I thought we got along okay."

He sucked in a deep breath.

"You were the only one I ever actually trusted."

Another breath. Against his broken ribs.

"In the whole mercenaries. I trust you, Logen. I trusted you."

All of the injuries he'd suffered these weeks finally hurt. His mouth swelled up where the teeth were loose, pulverized into his gums, and the hole from the last one gaped and bled copper into his mouth. The cracked ribs cut into his lungs. Fluid filled his sinuses, and all of his bones ached, and his skin stung from the raw, glistening patches rubbed off his wrists and ankles.

"What do you want from me?" he asked hoarsely. "You want me to say I'm sorry? I'm fucking gutted."

Her face flattened to acceptance. Bitter, angry, hurt acceptance. "I knew you'd confess."

"Oh, yeah?"

"This whole time, your face said you were guilty."

He jerked against the chains again, unable to rub the face that apparently professed his guilt.

Did he feel guilty? Of course. He'd been hanging out on his bunk while the woman he loved had been fighting for her life—and lost it. He might as well have opened up the force shield and done whatever else she'd said. He was the most useless backup in the history of backing someone up.

So now he'd really fucked up. He'd practically confessed. She'd leave, tell the Bad Company CO bastard, and she'd be left alone on the planet with the real murderer.

But she didn't leave.

"That's only my first question." She rubbed her face, looking even paler. "You keep saying you didn't kill me. So who did?"

Wait.

"You believe me?" he said.

"There's a lot of ways to lie," she said. "For example, you can slam a person's head into a counter, and then, when the cops ask if you gave me an injury, you can say

41

no, because actually it was the counter. See? Then that part's not a lie."

But that was more than anyone else had given him.

"Who is it?" he asked. "The other suspect."

"I don't know. I'm just asking questions."

"What did you spot? I'll rip his arms off."

She focused on his temples. "You sound awfully emotional for a man with a stent."

Fuck.

He tried to misdirect her from his feelings. "Someone is lying to you."

That grabbed her full attention. "Who?"

"There's more to this than they're letting you know."

"Who's they? Who are you protecting?"

He was protecting *her*.

"Why aren't you telling me? Are you under orders, or giving them? I can't protect myself if I don't know where to look for the danger."

He held her shimmery gaze. For now, he had to rely on her. Until he could figure out a way to make them believe his innocence. He had to rely on her to find out the truth for the both of them.

"Don't close your eyes."

Don't close your eyes.

The words rang in her head that night as she succumbed to pain and exhaustion.

Don't close your eyes.

Don't close them.

She spent the day in recovery, fighting to regain her strength.

Another danger lurked around her. Logen was one. The unknown was more dangerous.

The following evening, her team turned up in Medical in their suits for Upstairs.

"We've lost contact with the resupply drone and we're

heading to its last known location to make repairs," Vi announced.

"Shitty Hazard Zero equipment," Iren muttered over Vi's shoulder, dumping supplies into their bin while Navina directed him, inputting the inventory into a tablet.

"You are going to stay in Medical under care of your medic."

"I want to go to Base Two."

"In Medical, hooked up to the monitor, with three people on your six," Vi emphasized. "Not over to an abandoned base where we already turned off the force shield."

"We have less than a week to gather evidence before we're all in space and never find out who Logen's accomplice was."

Vi's eyes went unfocused.

Iren and Navina shared glances.

No fucking way.

"You already know who his accomplice is," Talia said.

"Accomplices," Navina said, emphasizing the plural.

But Logen thought it was only one accomplice, and he ought to know. Strange.

Vi nodded for Navina to explain.

"Logen hears voices," Navina said. "He received an order through his stents to kill you."

"You can do that?"

"It's how they control the prisoners. But this order came from the makers of the stents. The Robotics Faction.

The Robotics Faction was a mysterious group that produced nearly all technology. It was cheap, easy, affordable, ubiquitous.

She twisted the penknife. Like every other piece of technology in the room, it was printed with an RF serial number composed of Robotics Faction parts.

They also produced war machines. She had fought some of them back in Hazard Five. But the robots themselves were mindless and brainless, programmed to execute orders. It gave her a false sense of the intelligence behind them.

"The Robotics Faction wants to kill me?" Talia repeated. "Just me? Why?"

"Something about bad genes."

So she'd lost the genetic lottery. Somehow.

And robots had ordered Logen to kill her. Through his stents. She didn't even know it was possible.

Was the penknife trying to kill her?

It sat in her hands like a dumb, ordinary penknife.

Her head hurt. "Why would a military company put something in their soldiers' brains that could be controlled by someone else?"

"Obviously it was unplanned," Vi said.

"Take them out!"

"Stents can't be taken out," Navina piped up. "Your brain grows up around them, using them to grow in new directions, and you'd end up with severe brain damage."

"They can only be shut off," Vi said. "Which is what we're going to do to Logen's at the solar station."

If Logen had been mind-controlled by the Robotics Faction to kill her, then his body had moved on its own.

She had succumbed to a murder she had never seen coming. Which meant if she let down her guard, he could attack her again.

She could never, ever, ever trust him again.

"I'm sorry, Talia."

"It's fine." She was used to trusting no one.

The pity in Vi's silent gaze weighed down on Talia like heavy gravity. She was not a weak woman. She was not a victim. And if the Robotics Faction wanted her dead, she was going to give them a hell of a fight.

"Whatever he did isn't his fault," Vi said. "But it's better not to let him know that we know. He could still be transmitting back to the Robotics Faction."

"You're saying his stents are still working, and have been, the whole time?"

The women nodded. Iren puttered around the room, listening but not participating.

"But he thinks they stopped working." No, more than that. "I think they stopped working. I do."

Iren stopped. "Well, then, why did he kill you?"

Everyone looked at her.

"He's already a criminal," she said slowly.

"Aw, come on." Iren tossed his box at the door, rested his hip against her pallet, and threw his beefy arm around her shoulders. "That guy's only human when you're in the room. The instant you leave, he's a hunk of ice."

"A crime of passion can strike at any time."

"Passion? That guy?" Iren laughed in her face.

Navina and Vi traded amused smiles.

"It's possible," she insisted.

"There's no arguing with you." Iren patted her and let go.

"Don't argue with a spotter," Navina scolded.

He hefted his box. "Far be it from me to interfere."

Her head hurt again.

"I need to review the holos," she said. "And I need to go to Base Two. And if his stents really are still working, the obvious accomplice is anyone else with a stent."

Iren, Navina, and Vi traded glances.

"So it's obvious, like I said," Talia said. "Check everyone's files for prison time."

"It's not so easy," Vi said. "We don't have access to the classified files. Sirus had all of those."

And now he was gone fishing. "Bad Company has a CO."

"He's only in charge of us on this assignment, so he didn't get access to our permanent files before we left. After Logen's incident, he put in a request for ours weeks ago."

"And?"

"We got yours and Logen's so far."

She rubbed her head. "I know we're only Hazard Zero,

but what the fuck? Is anyone even listening to us at the solar station?"

"Well, that's the other reason to check on the resupply drone."

Talia dropped her hand. "Base Two is still an obvious place to investigate."

"We don't have the manpower."

"Let me and Daz go."

Navina bit her lip.

Iren shifted.

Vi took a deep breath and held Talia's gaze.

"What now?" Talia demanded.

"The re-supply drone wasn't empty."

"It was chock full of samples," Talia guessed. "And equipment, since we're heading out."

"And your restore point," Vi said.

No.

But of course it was.

"Those things are impervious to everything." Her voice trembled. Dammit. "They're indestructible."

"Stay in Medical."

"That's where they'd—"

"Please remember a mysterious, all-powerful organization of non-human robots is trying to kill you. They've already infiltrated *the brain* of your closest teammate. You don't know where they'll turn up next." She leaned forward, dark eyes glittering with deadly intensity. "They might come here personally to kill you."

Talia clenched the blanket.

But she couldn't let Vi see her fears or the smoky second would order something more draconian. "If they want to waste the fuel coming to the ass-end of space to cap one unlikeable woman, they've got more messed up priorities than the whole mercenary corps."

"Aw." Iren hefted his box onto his bulging shoulder. "You're likeable."

"Like a hellbender," Navina agreed. "Or one of those

adorable poison-tipped spiky lizards."

"Thanks," Talia said dryly. "You guys are the best. Too bad you won't be around to keep the jokes coming."

Or to keep an eye on her.

Vi narrowed slightly and leaned back. "Pleasant dreams. *In Medical.*"

So, Talia laid awake until midnight.

Every time she closed her eyes, she saw Logen. Beaten, bloodied, tied to a too-small chair.

The coldness of his face on those interview holos. The deadness in his expression looked exactly like Rezo the instant he reached for her with punishment in his mind.

They looked the same.

She shuddered.

Why think of this now? She had suppressed all those memories, and now they had started welling up, forcing her to look at them and remember.

She focused on the more important question. Who was Logen working with?

He was deadly. Dangerous, with a gorgeous lethal beauty.

Everyone knew she was confined to Medical. One well-placed missile and the whole wing would disappear into a crater. And her along with it.

Logen told her not to close her eyes...

After the roar of the Upstairs shuttle faded away, she woke Daz out of a dead sleep. "My med line is bothering me."

He stared at her, bleary in the darkness. "*You* want a sedative?"

"Turn off my heart monitor so I can unplug it."

He scratched his head. "Are you getting me in trouble?"

"Vi will never know."

He shrugged and showed her how to deprogram the all-base alarm. "So if she asks me, I can say honestly I did not turn it off."

She followed his directions. The heart monitor turned off.

He tapped something over her head and returned to his bunk.

Her neck started to burn. "What was that?"

He spoke through a yawn in the darkness. "Go to sleep."

Fucking sedative.

She yanked out the tube, ignoring the stab of pain and the hot warmth of blood, and lay with her legs in the air until the light-headedness passed. Then she realized she was still leaking blood all over the place.

Whatever.

She stuck a piece of pressure tape over the hole to keep from leaking out any more, climbed into her exoskeleton, and floated to the officer's ready room.

It was locked.

Since her identifying comm badge was still confiscated, she couldn't force it open. She was probably unauthorized anyway.

She headed to the mess hall. The reprocessor refused to dispense liquid, and she was too weak to argue with it. She had to wait until an insomniac biologist slammed a palm into it several times, and got it working again, before she floated over and got a coffee.

Alone with her thoughts, she sipped the bitter liquid and studied the shadows.

Maybe they did loom, dark and sinister.

A long, low cackle of a deadly dinozoid seared across the dark night sky.

Don't close your eyes.

He'd said it many times. Most recently on an archaeological dig, where raiders had tried to take out their clients, and their valuables.

On their last attempt, they lulled everyone into a false sense of security and then attacked while they were unarmed and unprepared, in the mess hall.

Well, except for herself and Logen.

As their acid bomb broke apart and oozed through the hall, sending the others running, he grabbed his backup pistol out of his jacket and started shooting randomly. She stopped running, jammed on her oculars, and leapt from table to table to reach Logen. He covered her to her last leap, when she crashed into him, and then he steadied her on the table with a powerful arm around her waist. She synced to his weapon and lit the targets, and he rotated with her in his arms, like a dance, firing on her marks.

Then, his powerful biceps had flexed to cushion her from the harsh kick of the old weapon. His iron-hard thighs had steadied her, anchoring them to the acid-smoking table. And his cut jaw rested lightly against her forehead, rough and sexy, taut as they moved in tandem.

With two split-second sweeps, the assault failed, stopped by the two of them.

All in a day's work.

Their employers had looked at him with awe, and at his stents with unconcealed fear, but she had only experienced an onslaught of raw physical desire. Here was a man she could anchor to. Here was a man who, at the height of danger, held her close and shot her targets. Here was a man she could trust.

"How did you know?" their employers had asked him, eyeing the stents. "How'd you know they'd come back one more time?"

But he didn't know. When their employers left, Talia had complimented him on his preparedness.

His expression had gone blank, which for him, was a relaxation from the perpetual scowl on his default emotionless face.

"I've got a good Spot," he said, making the desire pulse hotter. "We're not out of this yet. Don't close your eyes."

Damn him. Damn him, damn him.

Talia rested in the nearly empty mess hall, watching the darkness climb into dawn, and heard the jungle wake up with screams.

The Bad Company CO saw her before the first meal. "What's this about leaving Medical?"

"I want to visit Base Two."

He stared at her like she was crazy.

"I want to gather evidence."

"For what? He acted alone."

"Vi said—"

"You didn't get anything out of your Gun. Your restore point's in question. No way in hell am I letting you off Base One."

"Then can I review the holos again?"

"No."

"I might see something everyone else missed." Such as the evidence of robot accomplices she hadn't known to look for the last time.

The CO rested his lantern jaw on his big fist. His hand was healed, the knuckles shiny where new skin had been applied. He had beaten Logen for answers and she couldn't help hating him. At least Vi had stopped the beatings.

"Unlocking the door takes seconds."

"It's locked because my team's sensitive files are in there, and I can't afford anyone to babysit you."

"I'm not going to watch anything unrelated."

"You're not even a real mercenary yet."

"What can it hurt?"

"It's already a pain in my ass."

"But—"

"Contact me after you pass your physicals. And get back to Medical." He left.

She tightened all the muscles in her body, red and hot. She was naturally weak and had to put in twice as much effort to get strong.

Another reason she was so easy to kill.

Logen had said she must have fought. Damn right. She returned to Medical, started the physical therapy holos, and doubled down on her exercises.

Talia also persisted in bothering the Bad Company CO while the base was dismantled, generally increasing his ass-pains. She didn't have a hell of a lot else to do but jump at every shadow, snarl at the civilian biologists, and hate herself for her weakness.

"My team's rendezvousing with the damaged resupply drone today," she said, while demonstrating she could walk slowly now without the hover disk. "I have to spot for them."

"Spot what? There's only audio and it's delayed by six minutes on the shitty slow-wave comm. Besides, they're backed up by the main ship."

"I'll be one more pair of ears."

"And, when jack shit happens, you'll help yourself to those holos again."

She wrapped her hand around the medical monitor cable tying her heart beat to the base's alarm system.

"Fine. We're almost loaded. Watch with my spotter." He checked his chronometer. "There's a fog storm coming. I'm sending up the biologists ahead of it, and Chaelee's going with. You and your medic will come with the remainder of my team on the second trip. We're getting the hell off this cursed zoo tonight."

"I'm packed."

"You've got two hours."

She deactivated the system and tugged the monitor line free. "Thank you, sir."

He met her eye. "Plenty of time to prove that criminal bastard's irredeemably guilty."

CHAPTER 5

She sat beside Chaelee in the dim officer's ready room, studying evidence. Weather patterns, animal reports, ship sightings. Astrological signs.

"What's this ridiculousness about the Robotics Faction?"

"We received a transmission about it the day after you died." Chaelee played it.

"This is an emergency alert," one of the mercenary company's highly positioned generals proclaimed. "On Old Empire Date zero-six-zero-six, the Robotics Faction attacked without provocation the Antiata Hyeon home planet Seven Stars. They targeted everyone in possession of a specific gene."

One that Talia apparently had.

"Any soldier with a cybernetic stent is to be considered a potential hostile and sequestered immediately. The following sectors should avoid contact with all unknown ships."

It listed their sector.

"And that's it?"

"It came via an ancient communications technology and took days to arrive," Chaelee confirmed. "We haven't heard anything via our regular comms. That's why there's been no response to our request to send everyone's classified files. Nothing from the solar station."

"Are you sure the problem is with our comms?"

Chaelee laughed at her for even asking. "I think we'd know if the whole Antiata Conglomerate was under attack."

Shitty Hazard Zero equipment.

"Funny, isn't it?"

Talia was having trouble laughing. "What is?"

"The Robotics Faction wakes up one day and decides to wipe out everyone with this one mysterious gene. So, they activate Logen to kill you. Why didn't they flip on the two hundred science androids we have stacked in the back storage building? That'd unleash the robocalypse."

Fuck. She'd forgotten about those.

The biologists had tried them first, like usual, before being forced to pack them up and contract first Bad Company, and then also the Misfits, from the Antiata Deterrence Corporation.

"What is the Robotics Faction thinking?" Chaelee held out her palms. "If they killed everyone at once, there would have been no one left around to request your restore point."

True. "Well, they only care about killing my gene. Not everyone else's."

"What's a little collateral damage? We're only humans, so far as they're concerned. They're robots." She shook her head. "It doesn't make sense. Why only you? Why right now? Why this planet?"

All good questions.

"Maybe the robots need everyone alive for some reason."

"Like what?"

Okay, setting that question aside for the moment. "What if the Robotics Faction is going to use this planet as a base for taking over the solar system?"

Chaelee studied the maps. "They can't get too near the wildlife unless they want to end up in something's gullet."

Yes, that was the whole reason human mercenaries had been hired to guard the biologists on this expedition. The dinos couldn't leave their science droids alone. They were attractive metal chew toys.

"But it could be done."

"It would be easy to drop a couple of ships and hide somewhere. The fog is always dense in the Arctic." She shook her head. "Why would they want to take over this solar system? There's nothing here but us, a couple locked-down worlds, and a prison planet."

"The prison planet would be full of people with stents."

"But why... Oh."

They came to the same conclusion at the same time. The Faction could be using this planet as a base to take over the prison planet. They could create an entire mind-controlled human army made up of ruthless convicts, under control of psychotic robot overlords.

Chaelee shivered, then shook her head. "They'd have to get through the Wardens first."

True.

The only thing more terrifying than a prison planet was the aggressively trained, highly outfitted, entirely lethal cadre of Wardens policing the planet and its near space.

Talia saw nothing. She could see a pattern, but the pattern didn't make any sense.

"What does everyone else think?" Talia asked. "Your Nav, or your Second, or your CO?"

"They're all too busy packing up. Our next assignment is on sunny, civilized Vasso."

"Nice."

"Yeah, it's about to get less so. The new mineral rights owners are descending on the current inhabitants. It's hard to kick people out when the first squatters showed up ten generations ago. But at least it's no jungle."

Back to the current conundrum. "We must be missing something."

"Well, we're definitely missing something."

"We could at least send this theory on to the solar station."

Chaelee opened up a channel and shot the message. In six hours, by the slow bounce of their communications equipment from the surveying satellites ranged between this planet in the ass-end of space and the solar station slightly nearer an intergalactic Hub, they would get an answer.

She sat back. "Doesn't help your Gun, though."

"Where have we got for identifying his accomplices?"

"Nada. A fog storm rolled in that night, too." Chaelee tapped the screen to show the limits of the electromagnetic interference. "That's why the satellite couldn't record when the force shield went down, and we can't establish a time of death."

On another screen, they tracked the incoming fog storm currently threatening their Upstairs communications with the biologists' main science ship. For the moment, a low volume chatter between Navina and the Bad Company navigator hissed in the background.

"I think better when I'm eating. Protein bar?" Chaelee offered.

Talia liked Chaelee more and more.

She chewed the malformed bar, product of another open-palm argument with the mess hall reprocessor. It tasted like cheese and blueberries. "Any news on Logen?"

"His brother fixed his tooth."

So, now he'd go back to prison in one piece.

Talia polished off the bar. "What haven't I seen?"

"His classified file." Chaelee cycled through more holos.

As the only functioning spotter, Chaelee had watched them in order to advise her CO on anything he had missed. Talia debated requesting access. It was a hell of an invasion of privacy. She wouldn't want anyone digging in hers. No more than the higher ups already did.

More than anything, she wanted out of the mercenaries. She wanted to be a free civilian again. She wanted to live in a world where no one owned her, no one pawed through her past whenever they liked, no one told her what to do or how to live.

"Oh, and also his interview with you." Chaelee queued up the holo.

Talia stopped her. "I was there."

"You sure you don't want to see? I didn't have time to watch."

"He confessed."

"Yeah... I do have an alternate theory, if you would like to hear it."

They were coming up against the two-hour mark. Talia removed her oculars, set them on the comm panel, and said, "Sure."

"Say he actually is innocent. There are three damning pieces of evidence against him: The stents, the blood on his hands, and the fact that he killed a member of his team already."

What the fuck?

"What?" Talia said.

"It's in his classified files," she said, also glancing at the time. "It's the reason he went to prison and has the cybernetic stents to begin with. He killed his last spotter."

Fucking hell.

Their team was closer than blood, closer than air, closer than close.

The blackness swelled up in her heart and cascaded over her. A tsunami of realization. She couldn't catch her breath. The dry protein bar lodged in her throat.

She had been wrong. She had been so wrong.

"Take the blood," Chaelee said, not realizing Talia was done with the thought exercise. "Its smudge on his palms is consistent with having gripped something, like a log, that had your residues smeared across it. We found him in the woods, doing concentric circles outward from Base Two. Maybe he crossed the trail of an animal dragging your body without realizing it."

"Or he did realize it," she snapped, "because he fed me to a damned snakezoid."

"Second, the stents. He's never tried to kill anyone after the first time."

"That's what the stents prevent."

"Well, think about it. If the stents are shut off, the Robotics Faction isn't controlling him. He has no accomplices and he's acting alone."

"He killed his last spotter," she said.

"It's too much a coincidence, don't you think? If he wanted to murder you, he could do it any time. Not happen to do it the same week they issue a general warning about people with stents."

"Maybe he's taking advantage of the confusion."

"But we never told him about it. We didn't know until after your death. Are you saying he received the Robotics Faction kill order, shut off his stents, and then killed you?"

Fine. It was a coincidence. She returned to the important point. "He *killed* his last *spotter*."

Chaelee shook her head. "I don't know enough about his situation. But, I've been killed by my own team before."

"Accidents don't land you in prison."

"Logen wasn't court martialed. It could have been much worse."

"No offense, but you may not be the best judge when it comes to survival."

Logen didn't belong in Hazard Zero. A man with his talents belonged in Hazard Five, and his demotion was either because of the stents or because his brother had screwed up. Their contract was written so they were a matched set. If Daz ended up in Hazard Zero, Logen did as well.

But Logen had done something unforgivable. Not only had he committed a crime, it was the worst crime. He had killed the closest member of his team.

On purpose.

Gun and Spot. Spotter and gunner. They worked together, one picking the targets and the other executing them.

Funny how, in the beginning, she had thought it a mark of trust when he had stopped double-checking her work and shifted to automatic fire on the targets she selected.

All that time, he had been evaluating whether she should live.

"Yeah, I know," Chaelee agreed with her earlier statement. "I feel guilty every time I let my team down. I'd rather die a hundred times than let another person die once."

"You might do more good if you lived to fight another day."

"Well, so, we're back at Logen being the murderer." The two-hour timer went off. Chaelee stopped it with a sigh. "At least we got him, and the witch hunt is over."

Talia's investigation was over. She only hoped the Robotics Faction was to blame. Either way, she was wrong to have trusted him. He was dead to her.

All that virile masculinity. All of that quiet solidness. All of the man who stroked her dreams, slid into her desires and re-imagined the sweet future denied to her.

Dead.

Her muscles felt as heavy as granite pressing into the chair, despite the exoskeleton support.

A hundred centuries of merciless, lonely warfare stretched in front of her.

She would never escape the mercenaries. She would never see her family again. She would never find love. She would never, ever pay out and become a free civilian.

Her past was a dream. Not a dream, a lie. A lie teasing her about something that had never existed. Could never exist. Happiness had never happened to her, and would never happen to her, and could never happen to her.

And Logen was only the most recent illusion of her stupid, idiotic, weak-willed disappointment.

The shuttle roared as it took off.

Talia put aside her personal headache. "Weren't you supposed to be on the first shuttle, escorting the biologists up to the main ship?"

"Shit." Chaelee tapped her comm badge. When she couldn't get an answer, she walked to the door and shouted down the hall to one of the other Bad Company guys.

Because she had nothing better to do, Talia found the queued holo of Logen's interview with her and started it.

His strikingly hard, blank face stared at a recorder mounted above the door. At her entry, he tilted his head and squinted, and said his creepy line about moving forward so he could kill her.

And still, despite everything, she reacted. Here was a rugged, tough, gorgeous man who had killed two team members without remorse. Watching his lips move sent little shivers through her, and her desires ached. Why torture herself this way?

She reached over to turn off the holo.

Then, something crazy happened.

The back of her head appeared on the holo as she floated forward, into the recording area.

His eyes widened. Emotion swept across his face like an incoming tide, unstoppable. Relief, anxiety, concern. He softened, became more human.

She didn't believe it. Couldn't believe it.

Talia grabbed for the spotter oculars and double-checked herself. Hurt, surprise, resentment, longing. There, the emotions printed across the oculars, each one pointed out with undisputable accuracy.

"Hey," Chaelee stepped into the room, "can I borrow your badge com?"

"Mine's still back in Medical," she replied absently. "I haven't 'earned my suit' back yet."

Hour after hour of emotionless footage showed a cold killer. She walked into his cell and set off passion-sparked fireworks.

And, at the end, when he was warning her, fear.

This fearless man warned her to watch out for a storm and felt fear.

The recording stopped.

She took off the glasses again and rubbed her temples. "Chaelee?"

The woman didn't answer.

Why hadn't they made Chaelee review this? Talia had been barely able to stand; she spoke to Logen, and her vision had blurred so badly she could barely keep the tears out of her eyes.

But she *knew* his stents had stopped working.

Which meant the Robotics Faction wasn't controlling him.

...so he must have killed her for the same reason he killed his last spotter. Murder was inside his soul. He was evil, and she had missed his evil. She always attracted evil men. Right?

Thinking this way made her tired. She wanted a second opinion.

She raised her voice. "Hey, Chaelee?"

The other spotter leaned in the doorway. "Yeah?"

"I want you to see something—"

"Emergency." The comm crackled suddenly. "Hello, Base One, this is Navina on the Good Explorer. We are investigating the resupply ship. Something is very wrong. We have suffered a casualty. Spotter Talia's restore point has been destroyed."

"Oh, no," Chaelee gasped.

Talia's stomach dropped.

Without a restore point, she could die permanently and never wake up again.

"We have to get you into protective custody!" Chaelee rushed back to the door. "Five guards! You need five guards at all time until you get another restore point made."

"Please place Talia under the highest protection until we can return," Navina continued, echoing Chaelee.

Chaelee shouted down the hall, "Hey! Who's here? Somebody answer me!"

"Also, we see several unidentified ships hovering around you on the planet. We are hailing Base One directly because the main ship has stopped answering our hails."

Indeed, the chatter of Bad Company's navigator on the main ship, previously talking to Navina and to the pilot of the shuttle Chaelee had missed, had gone silent. Only a suspicious hiss of an open line remained.

Chaelee touched her badge comm. Maybe it was not as broken as she had thought.

"Some of the unidentified ships are within striking distance of the base," Navina continued. "Are you reading these ships? Answer, Base One."

They checked the map screens.

The skies overhead looked clear, aside from the electromagnetic fog storm rolling in. Once it blanketed the region, the satellite wouldn't be able to communicate with the base, and their location would be completely cut off from the biologists' main ship—as well as the small explorer shuttle piloted by Navina, Vi, and Iren.

But there were no ships on any screen.

"Why would they say that?" Chaelee asked. "And where's the other ship, and the shuttle that just left? And where is everybody? You have to be protected!"

Talia scooted over to the comm and depressed the button. "Navina, this is Talia. Hello?"

She counted the seconds for the signal to bounce up to the satellite, then streak through ordinary space to the distant explorer, and then to return.

"Base One, please respond."

"Navina, we are here. Hello?"

"Base One, please respond. Are you all right? Base One, I have downloaded the last visual snapshot of your location from the satellite, and your force shield appears to be down. Is anyone there?"

Navina was right. The usual bluish glow that kept out the animals and the elements was missing; the jungle seemed darker, more shadowed.

"Well, that's weird." Chaelee depolarized a window. "They should have turned it on again after the shuttle took off."

A six-legged gecko skittered across the window. They both jumped. Its poisoned tongue sizzled against the glass, seeking prey.

Chaelee peered around the gecko. "How do you suppose it shorted?"

A disabled force shield. Non-operational communicators. Missing shuttles. Mystery ships hovering overhead.

An attack on a distant drone drew away her team and left Talia without a restore point.

An awful picture appeared in her head.

Talia curled her empty hands into fists. Danger zipped through her veins. She lowered herself below the ledge of the comm. "Chaelee, get away from the window."

"Hmm?" She tilted her head at Talia. "Oh, no way. I think we'd know if we were under attack."

"Base One—" Navina started to say.

Iren's voice in the background screamed. "Shit, shit, shit! Breach! Incoming!"

"We are being boarded. Base One, our hull integrity has been—"

The transmission hissed.

Fuck. "Chaelee, get down!"

"I know, but I don't see anything!" She pressed her comm badge, then shook her head and started for the door. "We can't sit here alone waiting for whatever might happen. You have no restore point. Try the base-wide announcement system."

Talia swore, rose out of her shelter, and pressed the announcement button. "This is an all-base warning."

Her voice echoed reassuringly through the mostly empty halls.

"The force shield is down and we have lost communications with Upstairs. Secure your area and report to the officer's ready room immediately."

She released the button.

The room exploded.

A cliff-breaker missile had a distinctive, escalating, oh-shit-the-world-is-ending whine. Minutes after the shuttle blasted off, the whine jolted Logen in his chair.

Seconds later, it boomed against the gigantic comm tower.

Shit.

The tower listed, weakened metal screaming under its own weight, and then the shrieking rose to eardrum-piercing agony. A shadow crossed over the window ledge above, widening and darkening. A deadly wind compressed the air as the tower obviously failed in his direction.

Shit. Shit!

He lunged against the chains, striving to break the weld to the floor.

The sound accelerated and the shadow blackened.

No. Fucking. Way!

He strained with all his might. Beneath his feet, the concrete cracked.

The tower smashed through the shed, crumbling it inward. Shards rained down on him. Huge metal pylons ruptured the ground and shattered the concrete. A massive central pillar flew at him.

He dove forward, into the gap between buckling struts, yanking the chair free.

The struts sliced through the lower back of the chair and severed his chains like a pair of scissors.

He continued rolling, scrambling for openings, as the tower disintegrated around him. Soil geysered up and dust obscured his vision. He raced for the outer edge of the dirty mushroom cloud, fighting for freedom. For air.

A strut emerged from the dust, whistling past his forehead with decapitating force.

Logen ducked.

It grazed him, shoving him sideways, out of the path of another unseen hazard. He got back on his feet and burst through, running fast and hard across the debris-strewn ground. The mushroom cloud poofed and dissipated. He cleared it and ran free.

The base was in shambles. Not only had the cliff-breaker destroyed the comm tower, it had also annihilated the officers' quarters and caved in half of the main base. If the biologists and most of the mercenaries hadn't loaded onto the off-planet shuttle, casualties would have skyrocketed.

As it was, he only saw a couple of Bad Company mercs emerging from the mess hall wreckage, bleeding from head wounds and helping each other out the low windows.

He himself was covered in dirt and almost unrecognizable.

His chains hung from him, battered and ripped open; one was missing from his right ankle, and the left chain was severed after the first link. He shook his wrists and the two manacles fell off.

A gash on his shin he didn't remember glugged blood, and another poured from his forehead down his cheek. He wiped it away from his eye.

Another sound penetrated his consciousness: the pop-pop-zap of shatter rifles.

Shit.

He limped toward the armory. He needed a gun.

Around the corner, a sight stopped him dead.

Robots. Shiny silver androids, marching out of storage on their own.

What the fuck?

One turned on him and lowered its gun. The others all turned and oriented on him too. Red targets wiggled across his pectorals.

He turned and ran.

The robots fired.

He dodged into the base. All those huge, open windows in the rooms leading to the empty north-south main hall offered no protection. Androids swarmed after him, slowed by their budget construction, but inexorable in their pursuit. Shots burned the corridor.

He ducked down a western corridor and landed in Medical.

No Talia.

Shit.

Had he heard her voice just before the cliff-breaker? Maybe she was in the officers' quarters. Except they were half-collapsed by the missile. His jaw tightened.

He ripped open the cabinet. There was a med pack. He stuffed it in his torn suit pocket.

Beneath it was Daz's Silver Sig. Pristine as the day it came off the assembly line, fully loaded and ready to shoot.

Logen grabbed it.

His brother ran up to the window. Shirt torn, mud and blood plastered to his face, he had the wild look of battle. And he was trembling under the weight of a shoulder-mounted missile launcher.

"You made it!" His relief swept away as he turned to watch for enemies in the wrecked compound. "I thought you were dead."

"Where's Talia?"

Daz didn't know. "Come with me."

"I'll sweep for survivors."

"Then get out of there."

Logen jerked his chin at the missile launcher. "You okay?"

"I'm fighting fire with fucking fire."

"Sure?"

The only thing Daz hated more than carrying a weapon was using it. Causing the damage he'd only have to stitch up later hurt his brain, or so he claimed.

"Fine." Daz grinned with all his teeth. "These metal-plated assholes are ones I'm not in charge of reviving."

Understood.

Lasers blackened the window around Daz's head. He jerked back, glaring at the emerging androids, and leveled the missile. "Hurry."

Logen headed back for the hall. "Meet you."

"Save who you can."

Daz fired.

The whine smacked into something and a huge explosion rocked the ground. He stumbled away, across the parade ground, the cliff-breaker a heavy weight on his shoulders.

Logen dropped into the west corridor. The androids reached the corner intersection with the north-south hall. He turned on Daz's gun and rolled into the line of fire.

Minutes earlier...

The explosion flattened them.

A blinding, deafening light smashed through the room, shattering the window and slamming Talia into the comm. It lasted forever, and it lasted no time at all.

A white shroud encased her. For minutes, she lay on the comm, staring sideways at the gaping hole through the cement ceiling. Black smoke roared for the sky.

After a hundred years, she blinked.

It was hard to think with so much crushing silence.

Ears ringing, she forced herself off the dent her head had made in the communications panel.

Outside, a shrieking and cracking continued, like something gigantic falling across the parade ground.

Around her, the other screens blackened, cracked, and died. The speaker to Navina no longer hissed, its active light extinguished.

Talia's shoulders stung and ached.

She pushed off the remnants of the chair and tried to stand. After a moment, the exoskeleton activated and her hover disk engaged. She moved aside her shredded patient uniform and touched her shoulders. They glittered with embedded glass.

Chaelee rose from the ground with a groan, touching her head. Blood pooled around her fingers. "I thought I was a goner."

Her voice cracked. It was both too loud and unnaturally hushed, as though Talia's ears were stuffed with cannon padding.

The room shuddered violently and the north wall caved in.

Chaelee scrambled out from its path; Talia floated after her, toes dragging on the ground.

Outside, at the end of the hall toward the rear of the base—to the armory—something shiny and metallic walked through the open doorway and started down the hall.

"What the hell is that?" Chaelee asked.

Talia moved as fast as her hover disk floated. Weapon. Weapon. She needed cover and a weapon. "Who cares? Keep moving."

A red target appeared on Talia's shoulder.

Chaelee gasped and pushed her. "Get down!"

The gun pop-popped and an electric bolt zinged between them, raising the hair on the back of her neck and singeing her exposed shoulders.

They stumbled up and Chaelee dragged her through

the base, weaving between piles of wreckage.

A breeze blew through the compound, and dust. An odd stillness fooled no one.

Outside, flashes of movement told her they were no longer alone. But the almost-glimpsed shapes didn't move like soldiers. They cast human-like shadows on the far walls, and sunlight gleamed off metal. They moved oddly, like robots.

A barrage of shots popped in the distance, in the direction they were running. Talia stopped them at the mess hall in the middle.

"We need a plan," she gasped.

"Don't die!"

"I meant where to go." Running aimlessly would drive them right into their attacker's trap.

"Go to the hover bubble!"

Good enough.

She started forward again. A noise sounded behind her. She looked over her shoulder.

In the hall behind them, one of the science androids clamped a shimmering force-baton in its pincers. The baton gleamed with enough power to push ships and skyscraper-sized dinos.

"Run!" Talia yelled.

The android touched a table with the baton.

The table yanked out of the floor and hurtled toward her, metal twisting and shrieking with conducted force.

Chaelee dodged sideways. "Duck!"

The table winged Talia. She fell to the ground.

The android moved toward her, upending more tables and throwing them aside with catastrophic, crushing force.

Chaelee turned around and ran back to protect Talia. "Hurry! If we stay here any longer, they'll finish their work and we won't have the chance to get your restore point remade. Let's go!"

Talia went for Chaelee's gun.

But Chaelee, misunderstanding her reach, yanked her

forward, onto the ground.

The robot approached. Its force baton swung toward her head.

It was arrested by a gunshot.

The shot snapped the robot's arm backward. Another slammed into its head, denting it, and a third exploded its silver chest plating.

She followed the line of fire.

Logen stormed through the bullet-ridden chaos, an iconic silver pistol flashing in his skilled hand, determination setting his indomitable brow. His weapon created a force of gravity, shielding her and him. Shots zapped past them, missing. His dark eyes focused on her.

The day heated to a hundred thousand degrees. Fires and explosions highlighted his rough body, rippling muscles, and focused fury. He annihilated all threats. He saw her and nothing else.

Yes. She turned toward her gunner instinctively.

He raised his gun and fired.

She froze.

Behind her, another robot exploded. Its force baton crackled with deadly force, now muted by his protection.

He saw yet another behind her and shifted his aim again.

She shook herself and started for him.

Chaelee made a sound of shock and horror. "The murderer!" She scrambled for her gun and raised it at Logen.

"No!" Talia reached out to stop her.

Behind them, inside the mess hall, a robot fired.

Chaelee's head turned blue with an arcing band of deadly electricity. She stumbled. Her eyeballs sizzled in her skull, her skin blackened, fire lit in her mouth. Her body fell forward, dead.

The robot who had shot Bad Company's spotter adjusted

its aim with a whirring sound and centered its red target on Talia's forehead.

Fuck.

Logen raced forward, striving for the angle to end the robot before it ended Talia.

She dove toward Logen.

They fell into familiar survival patterns by instinct.

He caught her, yanking her hard behind the cover of the hall, and shot the robot, melting its face with his fury. It fell over, smoking.

His arm arrested her around the waist and his jaw brushed her forehead. Resolute, deadly. Waiting for her to spot.

But she didn't have her oculars.

More robots poured with measured, mechanical steps into the hall behind him, and more from an eastern corridor ahead. Others clambered into the windows on the distant east side of the mess hall and raised weapons, seeking his Talia.

Daz's Silver Sig felt too small to deal with this threat. They were about to be surrounded.

"Is there anyone else inside?" he shouted.

She blinked in shock. "What?"

"Is there anyone else here?"

Shots whizzed hot past their heads.

She shook her head. "I don't—"

Another red target appeared on her face.

He grabbed her to his chest and launched them sideways out the west mess window, onto the main parade ground.

They hit hard, and she cried out as she hit her shoulder. He rolled, trying to absorb the force as much as he could for her, and yanked her up.

She trembled in the middle of the parade ground, white-faced, gasping, and black dusted her face from the other spotter's death. The hover attached to her exoskeleton made a grinding noise as it fought to hold her upright.

The wreckage of the comm tower closed them in like a wall. In the building behind them, the robotic firing squad drew together. He moved indecisively, uncertain which direction to go.

Her lips mouthed something. "Hover bubble."

Shit. Of course.

He scooped her around the waist and ran for the hover bubbles. Parked beneath the comm tower, several had been crushed outright when it collapsed. Another two were missing. The last one hovered a few feet in the air and listed to the side, damaged. Its force shield blinked on and off.

They had no choice.

He skirted the wreckage, left her to rest against the ripped metal tower feet, and fought to right the hover bubble.

It fought him back.

The rounded bottom, sized to hold six full-sized mercenaries in their seats plus supplies, bucked and slammed into him, knocking the air out of his lungs.

He landed flat on his back, struggling for breath.

She looked down on him. For a moment, her image swam, separated by a line of spirit he could never breach.

Then oxygen went in and he gulped air, his chest violently spasming.

She was still looking at him. Hopeful, worried, hurting, and desperately afraid.

He sat up to face the hover bubble again.

Shots smacked into it, blackening the metal and popping the control panels with deadly sparks.

Shit.

She pointed at the enemies pouring out of the damaged buildings, crossing the field like unstoppable metal ants. "They're coming."

He abandoned the hover bubble, grabbed her hands, and ran into the jungle.

CHAPTER 6

Talia gasped between dry lips.

Ahead of her, Logen crashed through tangled vines. The air grew dark beneath the canopy. Behind them, the shivering branches closed off, grasping fronds snapping back into position. It felt like the jungle was one massive anaconda and it swallowed them whole.

Her gaze dropped to Logen's broad back. Powerful shoulders shoved through the growling underbrush, and the scarred shoulder blades flexed as he forced a passage for her escape. Despite his injuries, he moved with monumental determination to take her to safety.

They reached a small clearing. He bent over to catch his breath and evaluate where they were.

Having him with her once again calmed her. His powerful form moved so easily. She felt safe.

He saw her patiently waiting and pointed at an angle. "This way."

"To?"

"The Supply Depot."

The depot was days away on foot. They were practically naked with no gear. "Suicide."

"Better than staying around here."

Behind her, another cliff-breaker exploded the base, and another after that. The roars echoed like an angry beast, louder than the most frightening dinozoid.

"We can't possibly make the Supply Depot," she said. "I don't have any navigation equipment."

"It's this way."

"How do you know?"

He looked away to compose an answer.

Not an answer. *A lie.*

Goddammit.

She was wrong.

He had killed his last spotter. He was leading her off into the woods, away from anyone who might be left on the base. Talia was wrong about men. She couldn't trust him at all.

She eased away. The grinding hover disk dragged her feet across oozing green lichen.

He noted her movement, took a deep breath, and straightened. "Ready to go on?"

"Oh no." She held up her hands. "I'm going back."

"You can't go back."

"Don't threaten me. I'm armed to the teeth."

He didn't call her obvious bluff. "Going back is dangerous."

"I'd rather take my chances with the enemies I know than the one I don't."

His face turned cold.

She turned around to return to Base One.

He reached out. "Don't."

"Don't touch me!"

His outstretched hand arrested.

They stood that way for a long moment.

He finally lowered his hand. "They'll kill you."

"Well, then there won't be any difference between them and you."

His teeth clenched like white slivers between his taut lips. "I didn't kill you."

"Sure? You've got a track record for bagging spotters."

He sucked in a breath, and said, "The androids have infrared and they're armed. They'll kill you before you even see them."

"I'll see the danger. I'm a spotter."

"You didn't see the danger at Base Two."

"And you know because you made sure?"

"Talia."

"You're with them. The robots. You're one of them." She pointed at his stents. "They're controlling you right now."

"They who? The Wardens?"

"The robots."

"What?"

"The robots," she repeated, remembering too late that he didn't know anything about the warning. "The Robotics Faction ordered you via your stents to kill me. And now you're finishing the job."

"But I don't want to kill you," he argued. "Anyway, it doesn't work like that."

"What doesn't work like that?"

"The stents," he said. "They kill emotion. They don't give orders."

"The Wardens order you around."

"Their 'orders' are more like a compulsion," he said. "Like when you're so hungry you can only fantasize about food, or when you're so exhausted you can't keep your eyes open one minute longer. That's how the Wardens make us act."

"The Faction ordered you to kill me in your sleep."

He swore. "For the last time. I don't want to kill you, I didn't want to kill you, and I never will want to kill you."

"That's funny, because I'm getting the vibe you're ready to kill me right now."

"Throttle you, yes. Kill you, no." He waved behind them. "Besides, if I wanted you dead, don't you think I'd have left you on the overrun base?"

"I don't understand the twisted mind of a murderer," she said, even as the truth of his words fully penetrated.

He looked furious enough to want to kill her. The stents probably weren't operating right now. He wasn't under Robotics Faction controls.

All the more reason he was dangerous.

"I'm going back with the only person I can trust. Me. You go your own way." She turned away, lifting her feet laboriously, fighting with the exoskeleton and weakened hover disk, to stomp away.

He looped a finger in the shred of her flight suit, stopping her.

She swallowed the pain of her shoulders and glared at him. "What?"

He lifted his gun and fired.

The bolt flew right past her nose.

She jumped and screamed.

Something gigantic leaned out of the shadows and collapsed at her feet. An unidentified species of leathery, snake-like crocodile bristling with teeth, poisoned spikes, and more teeth. It had hovered in the shadows less than a hand's breadth from her nose and she had never seen it.

Now, a hole cratered the spot between its crossed eyes. It twitched and died, leaving a mountain of flesh up to her chest.

They both stared at it.

She was squeezing his arm. Dammit. The instant she realized, she let go.

He caught her hand. "We stay together."

His palm was warm and enfolded her in steady comfort. She felt the ridges of scars on his knuckles. All the places he'd taken shots for her.

She swallowed.

Logen's steady dark gaze burned with promise.

Fine.

"Give me the gun," she said.

His eyes narrowed. "Give me the hover disk."

Her mouth dropped open. Seriously? He knew she couldn't move without it, and it would strand her in the jungle.

"For checking our position." He pointed at the canopy. The hover disk would float him above the tangled mass of greenery and give him a pterodactyl's view.

Wait. "I thought you 'knew' the way to the Supply Depot."

A muscle in his jaw clenched. "I know the way generally. We veer too far and we could miss it."

The grinding sound of the weakened hover disk was audible over the ruckus of the jungle. "It will never hold our weight."

"I'll be back. You stay here."

"You're leaving me helpless on the ground with that?" She jerked her thumb at the dead crocodilian.

"You have the Sig," he said, as he reached out and turned her, examining the hover disk.

His hand rested on her waist, hot and possessive. She swallowed on a dry throat. Although she was not a dainty woman, his palm spanned her belly. He had always made her feel powerfully feminine.

He yanked something on the hover, and the engine hushed to silent. Her feet lifted off the ground, floating her up to eye level.

"What did you find?"

He held up a control chip. "Someone's been throttling you."

She swore. She'd barely been able to get away from the attack. "Dammit, Vi."

He threw it on the ground. "Or it was put on by the murderer."

"You were locked up."

He fixed on her. "I was."

She swallowed.

At eye level, his gaze burned, sweet and hot, and startling awareness pounded into her center. The kiss from three weeks ago flashed between them, as close as yesterday. The day thinned to the same reckless edge, daring her to close the distance, to cup his face, to give herself one more taste.

"Give me a reason to trust you," she said. "Why did you kill your last spotter?"

His jaw clenched and released. "It's got nothing to do with you."

"As your second spotter and possible victim, I'd like to make that determination."

"He accepted a hit. A couple hundred for me to ice a guy's wife and kids."

No. "You didn't."

"I refused and thought it was over." He looked away. His lip curled in disgust. "I was a naïve, naïve bastard."

"You took the shot?"

"He was the spot. We were in the heat of combat. He lit up the target."

For the first ten years, Logen double-checked every one of her targets. He made her so paranoid she triple-checked herself. What finally broke their stalemate wasn't the heat of battle. While on a routine escort mission, she had spotted some civilians in trouble and broke orders to call it in. Now she understood.

"One more thing."

He looked at her again.

"Admit your stents aren't working."

Shock cleared his features. "Yes. They are."

No way. When he told her about his old spotter, his face lit with fireworks. Mostly guilt and remorse, but also anger and sadness.

Emotions no stented soldier would ever be able to reproduce.

"Why are you lying to me?"

"I'm not."

"I know you are."

He started to clench his features in denial, but then

realized his vehement denial made her point, and quickly tried to act emotionless. "You're crazy. And there's no time for this. Give me the hover disk."

"You are a terrible liar."

Something rustled in the shadows behind them.

Logen drew her roughly behind him and faced the new threat.

A crocodilian twice as large as the one he had killed stumbled out of the brush on stumpy legs, raised its snout to them, and set upon eating the dead one.

"We'll go up together," she said.

Besides, if his stents were deactivated, he was not under Robotics Faction control.

Logen deactivated the hover and her exoskeleton. He held her against his broad shoulder as he widened the straps and squeezed into them.

"This is going to be a tight fit," he said.

"Oh yeah?" She tested him, leaning a little too close. "I'm sure you've heard that one before."

His dark eyes burned from under his brow.

The day turned sizzling bright.

He disengaged. "Hmm." He tightened the exoskeleton.

One massive thigh slid between hers.

Delicious friction eased and intensified her hunger.

The waist cinched tight. His taut belly pressed to hers and locked.

She curled her hands around the exoskeleton, unbalanced. "Maybe this is a bad idea."

"I could leave you here." He clicked the hover disk, still resting in the small of her back. They rose half a foot, bobbing above the mushy greenery. "I still can."

The crocodilian raised its spiny head. Guts dropped from its jaws. The predator slithered toward them.

"Go," she ordered.

He was already gripping the lowest vines and swinging them higher. The crocodilian fell away from them.

He climbed the bulbous, gnarled, twisting tree, hand-over-hand up the trunk. The hover disk assisted their ascent.

The tree was like its own ecosystem. Every hand-hold dislodged squirming critters, and every time they pushed through another layer of leaves, they startled predators living in the new strata. Some possessed more teeth and viciousness than the crocodilian. All made an incredible cacophony, a virtual wall of sound to hide their location from any robot trackers on the forest floor.

Logen carried her. Lithe and graceful, strong and unstoppable. He sweated from the heat. The biceps she longed to curl her fingers around bulged from exertion.

She tried not to focus on the hard power of his thigh flexing between her damp legs. Or his body pressing against hers, forcing her to feel every inch of his masculine appeal. Or the soft grunts of exertion, sending her forbidden ideas of teasing other noises from him with her teeth and her tongue.

Tracing the bead of sweat down his corded neck with her tongue....

"Tell me your stents aren't working," she said suddenly, to keep herself from doing exactly that.

He grunted. "Not gonna."

Well, then.

She leaned in to him and nuzzled his kissable ear. "Logen."

He sucked in a breath. "What?"

"Logen..." She teased the sensitive lobe with her lips, giving in to her long-held fantasies. "Logen, tell me..."

He gripped the branch, swinging in place. His voice roughened. "Quit it."

What a delicious catch. She flicked her tongue against his heated flesh, enjoying the quiver. "Or else what?"

He didn't answer.

She took the lobe between her teeth.

He groaned. "Shit, Talia."

The long, hard masculine length of him pressed against

her thigh. She gave herself greater license, spreading her hands across his broad back, dipping beneath the shreds of the uniform he had worn for his whole confinement. "Why don't you come clean?"

"You... are not... fair."

His hot, rough tension pulsed an answering heat in her blood. She wanted to cling to him. She wanted to strip him naked. She wanted him filling her up, with her legs squeezing him deeper, until the world disappeared in passion.

The strength of her desire shook her. She'd meant to force his confession and instead, allowing herself free rein unleashed her own true needs.

She pushed back, forcing a gap between them.

The heat in his gaze burned hotter than any denial of his feelings.

Perhaps it was okay she traced every rippling line of muscle with her eyes and salivated.

He and Rezo were not the same. They were opposite. Rezo went dead when he looked at her. Logen came to life.

That made it okay to imagine his scarred hands, rough and welcome, cupping her breasts and caressing her body.

Heat blossomed between her legs, and that damned desire twisted in sweet agony.

Logen continued climbing. They broke through another layer. The thick fronds fell away and the sky glimmered through, white between the final greenish-blue layers, promising.

"Tell me the truth," she said. "Your stents aren't suppressing as they're supposed to. Why lie?"

"A man with stents can't be guilty of a crime of passion."

"You aren't guilty." She shared with him everything they understood about the Faction's orders. "Whoever else has stents is the real murderer."

"You believe me?"

"Yes," she said.

They broke through the canopy.

Sunlight burst down on them, warm and soothing. The trees swayed gently, rocking them to and fro, and Logen held them to the top securely. Behind them, a curl of smoke revealed the final resting place of Base One. Glittering mica in the high atmosphere meant they were not showing up on satellite, even if the satellite passed directly overhead.

"Thank you," he said, finally. His voice was still a little uneven. He cleared his throat and started descending. "No one else did."

She traced the thick scar along his jaw. A violent firefight had put it there, and his thickest armor couldn't protect him from all the lasers.

"Well, they didn't have the benefit of seeing you change. You have real emotions for me."

His eyes widened. "No."

"Hmm?"

"I don't." He spoke too quickly, and descended rapidly into the canopy again. "I don't feel emotions."

"You just admitted your stents are malfunctioning."

"Yeah." He wiped sweat from his brow. "But it's different."

"How is it different?"

He wiped the sweat again. "It's not feelings. It's something else."

She rubbed her thigh distractingly close to his bulging masculinity. "Are you sure?"

"That's nothing."

"Humble of you to say so. Most men would boast."

He eyed her sideways.

Yes, she teased him for the second time in one afternoon. This time, she did it because she wanted to, and not to test him. "You took a hell of a beating for me."

"It happens."

She let her fingers trace the scar she had only looked at

before. His skin felt warm and firm beneath her touch.

He sucked in a breath. "Don't."

Enjoying how it affected him, she had no intention of stopping. "I almost believed your lies. You care, Logen. You have a cascade of feelings. So why are you trying to say that around me you feel nothing?"

One breath went by. Two.

Nerves stirred in her belly. She needed this answer. Her whole life depended on it.

He swallowed. His Adam's apple bobbed in his manly throat. "Because."

"Because why?"

His brows drew together. "You're important."

Her heart thumped. "To you?"

"To everyone. And you're my teammate. Yeah. You're the most important spotter. Spotter and Gun."

Wait.

She drew back. "Teammate?"

"Yeah."

"You get a hard on for all your teammates?"

He stared beyond her, out at the canopy.

"Answer me."

"It's nothing."

"You said that already."

"Nothing," he said more firmly, and moved them toward the Supply Depot. "I'd have a hard on with any woman."

"You didn't react when Vi or Navina interviewed you."

"Right now, it's only you, but it doesn't mean anything. It's like a twitch. Or one of those hit-the-knee things. A reflex. You're not special. It's a base, physiological reaction."

"A base, physiological reaction," she repeated. "Oh."

"That's all. I don't even like you."

He reached for a branch, missed it, and swung over the abyss. Contorting the exoskeleton, he swung the opposite direction and then made the next connection.

I don't even like you.

"It must be uncomfortable to be this close to someone you don't really care about," she said.

He shrugged. "No choice."

"You're pretty dedicated to your job, for someone you don't even like," she heard her voice say, as her heart fell all the way into hell.

Logen took them to the edge of a cliff by treetop, and then climbed down and into a cave in the middle of the cliff.

Talia pointed out pools of water to assuage their thirst, and which caves were occupied. Giant cave creatures stretched out huge necks crowned with mouth-tentacles.

When he released the exoskeleton in the center of the dry, shallow, empty cave, she eased away from him with a deep sigh. "Thank goodness. I couldn't take one more minute. Teammates shouldn't get too close."

It stabbed him in the chest.

Logen moved deeper into the cave, investigating every deadly nook and crevice.

Good thing he had reassured her that he wasn't too interested. If she remembered how personal his interest in her really was—if she knew the stents were allowing more than his physiological reactions through, and how strong those feelings were—then everything would break again.

Just like it had all those weeks ago, the night she died.

If she teased him with her hot little mouth the way she had up in the treetops, it was going to get a hell of a lot harder. His cock, his resolve, his promise never to bring up his feelings again... Just one more tug on his earlobe while her thighs squeezed his, and—

"Logen?"

"Yeah," he called. His voice echoed in the darkness.

She moved closer. Distrust tightened her voice. "You disappeared."

"I'm right here," he said.

"Don't go so far."

He finished his circuit and limped back to her, assessing his strength. Everything ached.

"Let's sit nearer the entrance," she said.

"We'll be more vulnerable to anything passing by."

"We'll also be able to see them. I don't like the look of the back wall. It's not solid. You don't know what's going to come out of it."

He joined her closer to the mouth. "Take off your suit."

She raised a brow. "Do you say that to all your teammates, or am I special?"

A sizzle of heat flared between them. His cock hardened to rebar. Her professionalism always kept a distance between them before. Now she'd lost it, and he was struggling to keep up.

"All of them," he said. "When they're injured on the shoulders like you are."

She pouted—*pouted?*—and turned away from him, and lowered her suit.

The red site made his stomach knot.

He was going to fucking kill whoever was behind this attack.

Using sticky forceps, he managed to remove the glass. Her body had already started to encase some of the shards, and it hurt to yank them out again. But better to get them out now than let them encapsulate or work their way deeper.

She endured his treatment silently, her hands clenching the exoskeleton until her knuckles were white.

"There." He used up the only spray of skin regeneration cream. "Maybe it won't scar."

She eased the torn collar up gingerly. "I don't have a problem with scars."

"You've got a pretty high tolerance for ugly."

"They're not ugly. The only people without scars are ones who have never lived. Scars are a sign of life."

Her comment eased him like a shaft of sunlight. He had never been good-looking, and now, by anyone's standards, he was horribly disfigured by a warzone of scars and the more recent beatings. But she didn't look at him like his nose had been broken thirty times. She looked at *him*.

She noticed the dried blood on his cuff. "You should have saved some for you."

He shut off the pain. "I'll heal at the Supply Depot."

Streaks of gold crossed the sky and melted into pale blue, then deep indigo. The sweat stuck to him from the hot day turned cold in the night, trapped by his thin suit, but he didn't want to take the ripped fabric off. It was his only defense against the jungle.

Safety suit. Force shield. Meal bars. Water hydrolizer. His brain ticked off the things his body craved as the day dissolved unwillingly into deadly night.

Something screamed in the cave above them. Snarls made Talia jump and edge closer to him. He held himself still, ready for action, but the snarls quieted and turned to suggestive crunching, and then more silence.

Her touch tingled against his bare skin where her hand was curling around his weapon.

A big fucking gun. That's what he wanted. Something that could open the whole cliff, like the powerful cliff-breaker, or maybe a step up, a hull-cracker. Something that went in a cannon and had to be bolted to a planet because otherwise the force of its blast would move a ship out of orbit. If he had that, then his near nakedness wouldn't matter. He would be able to protect Talia against a hundred alien predators and a thousand metal-plated bastard robots.

The snarls receded, but Talia didn't put the space between them again. He sat as still as possible. If he didn't move, maybe she wouldn't either.

She lifted her hand away, killing that hope, and chewed on her fingernail. "You know, it's too bad."

His thoughts exactly.

Then he realized she hadn't been talking about putting distance between them. "What is?"

"Hm? Oh." She let her hand rest next to his thigh again and leaned on it. Yes. "We should've skinned that crocodilian and taken it with us. The skin would be nice and warm, and the meat would last us weeks."

His mouth salivated, but his brain didn't like the idea of having raw, bloody meat hanging around. "It was probably inedible."

"No, that one was edible."

He looked at her.

Her profile was visible in the moon rise.

"I read the reports." She shifted on the hard ground. "We can eat most creatures, including insects and reptiles."

He did not remember, but he also hadn't paid attention. Anyone trying to live off the land in a jungle like this had bigger problems than keeping fed. But now they had solved the bigger problems, her foresight was going to be the edge that kept them alive until they hit the Supply Depot.

"Good memory," he said.

Her lips curved, but the beautiful fringes of her lashes made her eyes look sad. "I had this recurring fantasy that I outran Rezo and survived in the nature preserve until he was captured. Finding my own water, building a shelter, scavenging. First thing, I researched it on every new planet. Now comes the real test."

She was amazing. He laid on his bunk between missions and watched war holos. She was so determined, and such a survivor.

"This is no nature preserve," he said.

"Yeah, I know." She laughed softly. "I thought that preserve was such a wilderness. There, only two species could have killed me! And they were rare. I was much more likely to die from exposure."

"Exposure's a risk."

"Yeah." She sighed.

The night fell like a curtain and the unfamiliar noises were made more unnerving by the lack of light. In the distance, the moon glimmered like a pale warning.

He was fucking cold. But if she wasn't complaining, no way in hell was he—

She shivered.

He wrapped his arms around her waist and rested her between his knees. His arms cinched around her soft middle, seatbelt style, pulling her back against his chest.

She resisted. "What are you—"

"Cold weather bivvy," he said. "Can't have either one of us suffering from exposure."

"We're not really—"

"Shivering burns calories," he said. "You're healing and don't have them to spare."

His reasons reached her. After a long moment of silent protest, she eased back, resting against his chest, took a deep breath, and let it out in a long sigh.

That was when he realized his mistake.

She felt like a fucking dream.

Her cold biceps pressed into his, seeking warmth, and her own cold hands curled over his bare forearms. Her shoulder blades flexed against his pecs. That was all normal, like anybody would feel on a cold weather bivouac, even though hell, it was *her*.

But her feminine scent, of damp sweat and exertion, and the divot between her breasts rising and falling he could see from looking over her shoulder—and so long as it was there and he was here, he was going to look—and the sensual curve of her bare neck he wanted to nip with his teeth to hear her moan, and her heart-shaped ass pressed right against his slowly-pounding-to-life cock. That was the real problem.

Back when his stents first shut off around her, he had to run out whenever she entered the gym. He was always in there off-duty, doing about a hundred extra sets to force his mind off her and back on his pay out target, and in she'd come with some skimpy workout shit. She'd bend over to pick up a set of weights, and *fuck* her clothes would stretch tight against her heart-shaped ass, and he had to drop his sets and get out of there *right fucking now* before his loose workout pants advertised what he really thought.

He was supposed to be unable to summon an erection, but whenever she got close, his mind went to hell and his cock followed.

He shifted, edging the dangerous part sideways before she got a nudge in the kidneys.

She nestled against him, letting her head rest under his chin.

Her delicious scent curled under his nostrils.

He was going to fucking hell.

Breathe in, breathe out, breathe in. Don't think about how she feels, how she'd feel writhing, how she'd feel wet with my sweat—

"What are you going to do after you pay out?" Her question, innocent enough, made him twitch like she'd fired off a pistol. "Oh. Er, sorry. I'm still suffering hearing loss from all of the close-range explosions."

"Nah, it's fine." He brushed aside her hair. If they had a bigger med kit, they could put in restorative cotton and repair her injury. Her ear felt small and soft.

She stilled.

Fuck. He was forgetting himself. His touch was unwelcome. He clasped his other wrist. "I don't know."

"Get a cold beer on a hot beach?"

He smiled into her hair. "That's Sirus."

"Not you?"

"No."

"Then." She traced a tendon on his forearm, drawing a sensual line from elbow to wrist. Heat pulsed into his cock. "What about you?"

"I haven't really thought about it."

"Aren't you paying out after this mission?"

He shrugged, unconsciously squeezing her tighter at

the reminder she believed him. She shifted, and he realized what he'd done, and eased off. "I could stay on, make a little coin. Have something to start with when I got out."

"Saving up for someone special?"

"No one yet," he said lightly, his heart suddenly pounding in his chest like he'd run a goddamned marathon from the base to right here. "But, yeah, the usual stuff I guess."

"House, health, and kids?"

Yeah. That was the usual. "This job is the only one I was ever any good at. Might as well stick with it as long as I can."

"This isn't exactly an easy civilian life."

"Civilian life wasn't easy on me."

"Better to get a job with benefits where, if you die, they resurrect you for free."

"I'm not exactly a good risk for employers."

"Why not?" It took her a moment to remember. "Oh, because of the stents? You could get them covered. A skin graft takes five minutes. No one would know."

He wished they could be dug out. Not deactivated, but removed completely, scooping out the fragile neurons grown around them and dug in like a tree root wrapping around a water pipe.

Another deeper, more important thought reached him.

He lowered his lips to her ear. "You really don't think I'm dangerous, do you?"

She eased up a shoulder, ticklish. "To who?"

Talia looked up at him, her profile so sweet in the pale moon. Her eyes were full of faith. That alone was his answer.

"You."

"I don't think you're going to kill me *now*," she said, as though he were an idiot. "I've been in your clutches for hours."

He pushed it. "You don't worry about what I'll do when they deactivate the stents."

"They're already malfunctioning. Once they're shut off, you'll be free to feel things."

His chest squeezed.

Fucking hell.

He leaned close, until their cold noses almost touched, until her breath caught and she swallowed. "I already feel things."

She blinked and licked her lips. "Physiological things."

Arousal pulsed in his blood. He nuzzled her. "Mostly."

Her breath caught again. He nuzzled along her silky jawline, teasing her creamy skin. There, the pulse of her body heated to match his. He pressed his lips to that hollow. She moaned.

It was the sweetest sound, and it laced his blood like alcohol.

He followed the sweet, hot flavor to her lobe. Taking the flesh between his teeth, he delicately tugged.

She moaned again and eased back into his embrace. Releasing him to do as he wished. Opening herself to his hot invitation.

He sought her mouth.

She opened to his hungry kiss.

Her mouth was blazing hot, wet, and slippery as their tongues touched and caressed. He squeezed her. She teased him, nibbling on his trembling lips. Making promises about what else her mouth could take in. Fucking hell. His tongue plunged into her, plumbing her secret depths. She grabbed his head and urged him on.

Her breasts brushed his forearms. He rubbed the heated globes. They were cool on top, leading to a pebbled point, and beneath where they rested against her ribs, they burned with a secret fire.

He palmed the soft flesh. She gasped and arched her back, pressing her hot flesh into his hands. His thumb brushed the pearl. She made a soft, inarticulate cry. He did it again, following her lead, bringing her to a hot, gasping edge of desperation.

He dipped below the collar of her suit.

She grabbed his hand, stopping him. "No."

He stopped immediately.

They both stopped, gasping. His heart thumped, his cock pulsed, his blood roared. Beneath his hot palm, her heart fluttered in her chest.

He pulled her back against him, hard.

She resisted, but then melted into his embrace, sealing their sudden flare of heat into the warmth between them, warmth to carry them through the cold night.

He understood her wanting to stop. They were in the middle of the fucking jungle. And she still had a head full of doubts.

The other part of him pulsed, telling him yes, they were in the middle of the fucking jungle, and he better do something about her doubts now, now, *now*, before he lost the chance.

No. He was protecting her now. There would be another chance. Many more chances. He held her close, rested his chin on her head, and breathed the sweet warmth of her silky amber hair. His hands squeezed her.

She shifted and let out a long sigh. "Your hands are cold."

"So are yours."

She let him thread their fingers together, trying to conserve warmth. "Hey, Logen?"

"Yeah?"

"If your cybernetics get fully deactivated, will your physiological reactions go away too?"

The chill of the night walked across his arm like foreign insects.

He shook it off. "No."

"No, I guess they would only get stronger. And you'd have reactions for other women, too. Or, wait. You said you already did."

She slowly stiffened. Then, she leaned away.

Fuck. "Talia, I swear to you, I'm not a dangerous—"

"Sure you are," she snapped. "It'll be great when the stents are deactivated, and you can have these 'physiological reactions' with whoever you want, and not be limited to someone convenient like me."

"You're not convenient."

"Great, I'm not even convenient. I'm just who you're stuck with right now."

"Talia..." He tried to pull her stiff back against him and melt her once more. "You're the only one I want."

"Right now. We covered that."

"Not just right now. Trust me."

"The last man I trusted blew my brains out."

How to convince her? If it weren't so dangerous, Logen would probably take off and let her anger cool, but he didn't dare let her go in this deadly cave. He had to face her glittering anger and draw it closer to him.

"You," he said unsteadily, "know me."

"I thought I did, but all you've done since I woke up is lie to me."

"You want it this way. Trust me."

"You don't trust me, so why should I trust you?"

"I do trust you."

"What happened that night on Base Two?"

Damn.

"See?" She hunched away.

"It was nothing," he insisted. "There's nothing to say."

He had promised her that night they would never talk about this again. He would uphold his promise even if she got in his arms and he forgot all the rest.

"Fine." She stopped him with one question. "What's happening to us right now?"

CHAPTER 7

Talia waited for an answer Logen refused to give.

"Nothing," he repeated, his face telling her certainly it was not nothing. "It's not important. You don't want to know."

She knew it.

And until he could trust her enough to tell the truth, she wouldn't trust him. Not really, not deep down.

Not with her heart.

The night passed and dawn arrived. They drank from the dripping cliff-side pools and shared the exoskeleton again. Logen climbed down the cliff and up the other side.

She squinted into the burning sun and stifled her yawn.

"You can sleep," he told her, sweating as he maneuvered up the cliff.

"That's poisonous," she pointed to the slimy lizard he was about to brush away from his next handhold.

He paused.

It opened its mouth and revealed a poison-tipped blue tongue.

He moved sideways, giving it a wide berth. "After we reach the treetops."

In the sunny open air, it was easier to hope Vi, Navina,

and Iren had fought off the incoming ships and were returning to rescue them.

It was easier to believe Logen's silence in the past was stiff-necked pride rather than unwillingness to trust.

Overall, it was easier to forget the things she disliked and concentrate on the things she liked. Such as a man's steady heartbeat thudding against her hand where she rested against his broad chest. The last time she had been able to rely on that sound had been holding her baby brother to her chest.

She took a deep breath, shaking herself back to the present. "I don't want to miss the Supply Depot."

"It's a huge clearing," he said. "No one could miss it."

They almost missed the Supply Depot.

In the mild afternoon, something orange flashed in the distance, off to the left. A marker from one of the collection sites she had missed while resurrecting? She puzzled over it while Logen continued on his way.

And then it hit her.

"That's it." She pointed into the wall of foliage, now requiring him to go back and see. "We're a few degrees off."

He swore and back-tracked.

"Amazing," she said. "You should've been a Nav, not a Gun. Did you always have this good a sense of direction?"

He snorted. "No."

"What happened?"

He grew edgy and shut his lips tight.

More secrets.

More lies.

"Glad to see our trust issues are behind us," she said dryly.

"I trust you with my life."

Interesting. Even without her oculars, she could see his clear-eyed gaze was telling the truth.

"But not anything else," she guessed.

His jaw tightened.

He reached the edge of the clearing, which from this distance did not look clear, and began his descent. Breaking through layers of foliage, they disturbed deadly alien creatures as they dropped from the open skies to the close-knit floor.

Twenty paces away, the concrete Supply Depot shed stood like a single tooth in a bare earth mound. Its shell bleached white and door mouth gaped, hiding dark, lurking shadows.

Logen extricated himself from the exoskeleton and crouched in the fronds, which reminded her to get the hell down too. They were still in shadow, and no sign of the androids or other enemies.

Or friends either.

"It looks quiet," she murmured. "Too quiet."

He nodded, his eyes cold. When evaluating threats, they were always on the same page. "We don't have many options."

They didn't.

A hostile jungle surrounded them and an eerily silent Supply Depot sat in front of them.

She reached for the gun. "I'll cover you."

He stopped her. "I run in, grab whatever gear I can find. You stay out of sight."

Sounded like he was going to get himself killed. "What about the androids?"

"Not concerned."

"Why the hell not?"

He pointed to a dismembered metal foot resting against the side of the Supply Depot. Fuck. If they had already reached here, they could be anywhere.

Someone else had already been here too, fighting them off. Possibly one of the Bad Company mercs. She silently hoped it had been Daz. It could have been anyone.

Anyone except one.

Rest in peace, Chaelee.

Chaelee would be resurrected, again, but she wouldn't

have the memories of sitting with Talia in the officers' room, scanning holos and joking about the myth of enhanced satellite images. Their camaraderie was gone.

If Logen died, he'd lose all the memories of rescuing Talia, of taking beatings for her, of fighting his own fight for her.

Her gut tightened. "I'm going with you."

"No."

"Anyone could be watching. Or they could have set up a trap inside the Supply Depot. The only thing we can be certain of is no one's watching us from orbit."

He followed her glance up at the white sky. A continuous layer of impenetrable, high fog blocked out the sun, but didn't diminish the watery heat.

"That's why you stay here." He evaluated the eerie depot.

"Logen—"

"Come and get me if something goes wrong."

Damn.

"No stupid chances," she pushed. If he died, she'd be all alone. "We all go home."

He nodded once, short.

Her throat closed.

"I've got you covered." She patted his back twice. His rippling, masculine back. A soldier going to war for her, entering a situation that could turn deadly. She let her second pat linger too long, then released him.

He caught her hand.

She steeled herself to apologize.

He pulled her hard against him and met her lips for a deep, soul-filling kiss.

Pulsing heat coursed through her, bringing her to instant awareness. Her hard nipples pebbled against his masculine chest. She cupped his cheeks and melted into him.

His tongue plunged into her mouth. Sweet desire twisted in her center. She needed him. His trust, his faith, his strength. She nipped his lips and nuzzled his rough, masculine cheek.

His wide palms spanned her hips, pressing her softness to his hard erection.

"Physiological reaction?" she asked, catching her breath.

His eyes darkened and he rubbed against her. "Like a sneeze."

Her body slicked, ready for him. "Bless you."

His lips curled. He kissed her forehead, squeezed her once more, and released her gently. So careful, for all of his lithe power.

Yes. His kiss filled her with strength, with power, with confidence. She was a fighter. She was going to survive. They both were.

He looked revitalized.

And deadly determined.

He checked their positions, ensured she was ready, and disappeared into the brush.

She deactivated the hovers and crouched in the mud. Her skin still smelled like him, soaked in his scent. She wiped her mouth.

Fuck. She'd forgotten the gun.

He reappeared at her side and held out the weapon.

She took it.

His cheeks still tinged and his eyes darkened, still wild. "Cover me."

"I already am."

He disappeared again. She watched for his movement against the foliage around the edge of the Supply Depot, but he was good. And there was no movement within it, either.

She squatted on the wet grass, her heart thumping hard against her chest. His kisses blew away her doubts and shone light in all the dark places. Another century in the mercenaries would be bearable if they could remain together like this.

If his lies peeled away to reveal the vulnerable core of truth.

And if they both survived.

Logen snuck around the edge of the Supply Depot as much as he could in the impenetrable vegetation.

He kept Talia's position in the corner of his eye as he moved.

She hadn't rejected him this time. Not only hadn't she rejected him, she drowned in his kiss.

Her responses, that she wanted him and more, kept his hopes alive, even as she called him a faithless player. He wasn't a fucking idiot and he knew his own feelings. If the stents got shut off fully, he'd only love her more.

But yeah. The way she grabbed his head and yanked him down to her, or teased him with a smart comeback and a little smile, or cracked open her protective shell and melted into his arms ... had she had changed her mind about him? Maybe they had a future together this time, as soon as he got her out of this mess.

Beneath his feet, jungle creepers slithered across the ground, covering over the ragged edges where once a force shield had held them back.

The shield had gone down yesterday, it looked like.

He reached the opposite point around the bare field and looked into the building. The jungle held its breath.

He stepped forward until he was visible and communicated the all-clear gesture.

Talia also emerged from the jungle.

He grabbed a rock and tossed it up in a gentle arc. It landed on the ground in front of the building and bounced.

A low, ominous wind blew through the depot. The empty doorway gaped, its interior shadowed.

Talia tossed a rock harder. It arced onto the roof and clattered down. They both waited. Nothing happened.

Fuck.

He took a deep breath. Psyching himself up for the long walk in the deadly open.

Across the field, her eyes fixed on his. Their worries matched.

If they had their battle gear, clearing a compromised area had a routine. They'd test as much as they could remotely, with robots, before going in. They'd test for holo-cameras and booby traps, and all the triggers: body-recognition bombs set to blow up when they sensed humans in proximity, facial-recognition weapons targeting only certain faces, scent-recognition triggers, the whole shebang.

Talia scanned the surroundings, covering him with the Sig.

Now or never.

He stepped out of shadow, into the field.

Standing exposed to a sniper's bullet or hidden enemy heated his brain for one long, hot moment.

Nothing happened. Still.

He let out his breath and walked cautiously toward the depot building. A hover bubble's landing gear had dented the ground. His ears strained for the deadly click of a pressure mine or the transcendent snick-whoosh of a charging laser pistol, the rolling pop of a contact-grenade, or the destructive whine of a cliff-breaker missile.

He moved into the darkened room. It took a minute for his eyes to adjust. Then, his gut clenched. He smelled blood.

An instant later, his stents kicked in and swept away the gut-clenching feeling. The familiar menthol coolness was both strange and unwelcome.

Someone had torn through the survival gear. The water filtration system was in pieces and the box with the emergency comm and spare parts was gone.

Fuck.

He stepped past the spilling open closets and cabinets

to tour the main and secondary rooms. Destruction everywhere, and a dark spray of biological tissue, but no body. He returned to the main room and sorted through the supplies.

The exposure suits all had long rips through them, destroying their integrity and making them no better than ordinary cloth. He found the knife amongst them and curled his fingers in the knuckle grips.

Sabotage.

Which meant someone expected him to come here.

Someone was there. With him. Right now.

Someone he needed to kill.

Hair rose on the back of his neck. The sense of being watched crept up on him. Anyone could be hidden nearby, wearing a chameleon suit, invisible until the right moment.

He stuffed useful supplies into a bag. He needed out of here as fast as possible. Talia was waiting on him.

A shadow moved outside the main windows. Boxy and metallic.

Shit.

He crouched down, lifting the knife to ear level, and crept forward.

The shadow hesitated.

He waited. His ears attuned to their footsteps. Soft, quiet, careful. Sneaking up on him.

The shadow stepped to the door.

Kill.

He burst from cover, bashing into the soldier and landing full force on her. She cried out and hit the ground. He brought the knife down decisively.

At the last minute, he registered it was Talia.

He diverted his hand and buried the knife in the dirt next to her head.

Her mouth flopped open, the air knocked out of her. Fear widened her eyes.

It sliced open his chest.

His own heart suddenly thundered in his ears, heat

rolled over him in a wave, his palm slicked as he yanked up the handle of the knife buried in the ground, and fury exploded from his mouth. "Fucking hell, Talia!"

She shook her head, still struggling to take in a breath.

He got up off her, and scanned the jungle while she finally sucked in huge, desperate, shuddering gasps. Sunlight reflected off her metal exoskeleton. Insects buzzed in the filtered white sunlight. Uneasy wind susurrated through the shadowed fronds.

They were out in the open.

He reached over to haul her into the shelter of the Supply Depot.

Her eyes widened further and she tried to move away.

Fuck!

He grabbed her by the exoskeleton and yanked her in, away from unseen eyes. Once inside, he released her. "What are you doing here?"

She crawled away from him, settling across the room, under a window. Her hands trembled. "I thought I would spot for you."

His hands were trembling too. He found a holster for the knife and attached it to his tattered belt. "What the hell were you thinking? I can handle this."

"I never said you couldn't." Her tone rose to a whine.

He stopped.

That didn't sound like his Talia. Near tears, her red-rimmed, frightened eyes and her continued shivering did not sound like the bold, strong, determined woman who stood firm and shouldered a world of challenges without asking anyone else for help.

He took a deep breath and let it out slowly. "Sorry."

She shuddered, not seeing him.

He needed to ground her. Without touching her, because she was still too sensitive, he needed her to reach for her own inner core.

"Where's the gun?" he asked.

She blinked.

Then, frowning, she patted herself. Locating the gun in her side holster, she held its long barrel, staring at it. Her breath smoothed and lengthened. Her shivering stopped.

Yes. She was strong and fierce and capable.

A few seconds later, she focused on him. "What did you find?"

"Not a hell of a lot." He tossed her the bag, then pawed through the remaining gear, separating it into piles of things they could use and things they couldn't.

One pile was a hell of a lot larger than the other.

She joined him on hands and knees, picking through the discards pile. "All the suits have been slashed."

"Hell of a sabotage."

She sat back on her heels. Sick understanding crossed her features. "Someone expected us to come here."

Their conclusions matched.

"Don't open any closets or cabinets," she said, studying the distant blood sprays. "I want to inspect them."

Before inspecting anything, she had to get into an outfit offering some protection. He tossed her a nicked exposure suit. "Put that on."

She moved away from the windows, stood, and set the gun and her hover disk on a shelf. Laboriously, she undid the exoskeleton, eased out of it, and began changing.

At the flash of creamy skin, he hardened to granite and turned away. Just like back at the gym.

Before the bonfire all those weeks ago, he'd seen her body thousands of times, but it hadn't meant anything.

Now...

The reflection in the cabinet mesmerized him.

Her body was sweet and soft, as he knew from so recently tackling her, and he wanted her squirming beneath him and dragging passionate fingernails across his back while she screamed his name in ecstasy. Delicate breasts, grippable hips, and that heart-shaped ass he wanted to squeeze and cum all over. His cock pulsed, throbbing with imagined pleasure.

He rubbed the dull surface casually.

"Like the view?" she asked, her voice amused.

He jerked. She'd noticed him looking in the reflective surface. Fucking spotter.

But it relieved him to hear her sounding normal again. "If I say yes, are you going to pound me?"

"I have a better idea."

At the hint of purr in her tone, he turned.

She studied him with a burning gaze that turned hotter. "You change too."

He lifted a brow. "You don't want to see this."

"It's only fair."

He indicated the scars. "Serious?"

She nodded at the suits on the concrete in a pile. "Go ahead. I'll watch."

He reached for his belt and tugged. The frayed fabric snapped, and his suit fluttered loose.

She licked her lips.

Suddenly, the concrete bunker was a hundred thousand degrees.

He hooked his fingers in the collar and peeled it open, revealing his massively scarred chest, and the dusting of hair that persisted in growing down below his navel, and lower. Her gaze consumed him, burning everything it touched. He kept peeling back, stepping out of the suit in bare feet and straightening to reveal the proud cock that sprang from dark curls.

Her chest rose and fell. A high blush colored her cheeks. "T-turn around."

He did, facing the cabinets. Displaying his scarred back, his bullet-ridden buttocks, his laser-raked thighs.

"Keep turning."

He did as she asked, turning full circle to face her again.

Her lips parted. She struggled to remain casual.

He helped her, tossing her words back at her with the same sardonic twist. "Like the view?"

She nodded, first slowly, then decisively. Her clear eyes

met his. "Yes."

It sucker-punched him.

She spoke without fear, without revulsion, without guile.

That was Talia. She always saw past the outside—past the stents, past his mistakes, past the scars—to the man. The man he was inside. The man he wanted to be.

That was why he loved her.

That was why he endured weeks of beatings and lost teeth to stay beside her.

That was why nothing else mattered. Not their hopeless situation, not what everyone else thought, not his impending court martial. He would protect her to his dying breath and beyond it. He would protect her forever.

And he would protect her from his feelings, if that was still what she asked of him.

She swallowed. "Um, I guess, though, you should dress."

He stepped into a slightly slashed suit and adjusted it, affixed his knife to the new belt, and cinched it down.

"There's a hole in mine," she noted.

"Pressure tape's right here." He turned and opened the cabinet.

She jerked up, from where she was cinching down the exoskeleton again, with a gasp. "No!"

Something round and black dropped from the top of the cabinet, where it had been precariously balanced, and fell to the ground.

Shit.

He leaped back.

It rolled into the empty clothing. Sensing it hadn't made physical contact with a target, the contact grenade popped upright like a piece of popcorn and flashed a purple light. It scanned their chests and made the iconic beeping. Three, two, one.

Kaboom.

He was already moving.

Grabbing Talia around the waist, he dove with her out the window.

The force of the explosion slammed them into the ground. Logen rolled atop to cover her. Debris puffed out the window and dusted them.

Additional contact grenades bounced out of the cabinets, pooling on the concrete floor. He saw a brilliant purple strobe and heard furious beeping.

Again, he yanked her up by the exoskeleton and started running, dragging her.

The crack-crack-crack-boom of combat grenades exploded.

The whole place went up, the entire structure, cratering with a sustained crack-a-boom that took out the entire depot. He ran, dragging her, and reached the edge of the clearing when a larger shockwave knocked them flat. Ash misted them, along with rubble and plastic shards. No joke, someone was trying to kill them.

They moved into the jungle, far from the smoldering disaster before the bomber came to check on their handiwork.

CHAPTER 8

Deep in the dense, tangled jungle, Talia clung to Logen as he finally stopped running.

He let go of her hand and she collapsed in a mulchy, flat spot. Behind them, the crackle of destruction echoed through the jungle, and smoke chugged into the sky.

"They definitely saw that above the canopy," she gasped, wiping hot tears from her debris-gritted eyes.

"Yeah, but who's 'they'?"

Hopefully the Misfits, and not only the hunting androids.

She rested while Logen reviewed their scavenged supplies. It wasn't much. A few meal bars and their suits.

They'd lost the gun.

They'd lost her hover disk.

Not only would they be slow, but they would be land-bound, too. Land-bound in the most difficult, uncharted wildness.

Hopelessness overwhelmed her. The shivers started in her belly. She tried to hug herself, to force them away like usual, to hide them before her team noticed. But they wouldn't stop.

"Hey." Logen touched her shoulder. "We made it."

Her brain refused to process she had almost died a second time, but her body had already long come to terms with it and gone to deep, primal emotions.

"Hey," he said again, and rested his large, warm palm on her fragile shoulder. "Hey, we survived. Base Two is still out there. We'll wire up their comm tower and call for help. We can do this."

She shook her head, still shivering. "It's so far."

He looked away, ashamed of his failure to notice the trap. She herself had been in the Supply Depot half an hour and also noticed nothing.

What else would they miss? How many more close calls could they handle?

They were going to die. Her and Logen. Especially her.

He had taken her down so easily outside the Supply Depot when he mistook for an enemy. She hadn't resisted. All those years of combat training and she was a failure.

Fear swallowed her whole and choked all the way down.

"We can make it," he said. "We're a team."

"Without your gun," she continued, hating the warble in her voice, "or my oculars, we're nothing anymore."

He frowned and looked away.

Proving her point exactly.

"I should never have left Base One."

"No choice." He tried to encourage her again. "We can do this. We'll move on."

"Who's 'we'? I mean, there's nothing uniting us, right? You have your stupid whatever 'physiological reactions' with no feelings. You're only here because you owe it as my Gun." She sank deeper into the mud and covered her face with her hands, blocking out his depressing resignation. "We go on and we're going to die, and I can't be restored."

"What do you mean, you can't be restored?"

Oh, of course he hadn't heard. She dropped her hands only after she was certain she had control of her lancing tears.

"My restore point was destroyed on the resupply ship."

"No."

"Yeah. They suffered a casualty—"

"No."

"Yes," she insisted. "There was a problem with the resupply drone. Vi, Navina, and Iren went to investigate, and they found a hole in the side where someone had bored in and ripped the restore point out, setting it adrift in space."

"*No.*"

"It was destroyed by the same Robotics Faction—"

"No!" He jerked to his feet and stared down at her, face red, hands flexing. "It's not true. They just restored you."

"Obviously," she snapped. "In fact, restoring me is the whole reason my restore point was ever removed from its secret, hidden hospital barge... Oh."

Of course. The Robotics Faction ploy was so obvious now in hindsight. Where was Chaelee? She had to tell someone who would understand.

Instead, she settled for Logen. Holding her forehead, she played out the theory in her mind. "The Faction activated someone to kill me, thus drawing out my restore point, and then they destroyed it as it flew back."

He whitened. "It's a lie."

"I'm under a death sentence."

"No, no, no! You are going to be fine. This is fine. We are not stranded in an alien jungle with two crates of androids hunting us while you have no restore point."

Somehow, his angry denial made it easier for her to deal with the terrifying truth. "Sorry."

"No." He shook his head and started pacing. "No. Just, no."

"Logen—"

"No!" Rage filled his bellow. "You are *not* telling me I could lose you forever. That's not possible. You're the only woman I've ever—"

He broke off abruptly, studied her for so long the tendrils of heat curled in her belly and warmed her like an embrace.

She swallowed a suddenly dry throat. "The only woman you ever what?"

He dropped to the ground without answering her, packed up their meager supplies, and started back toward the column of smoke that had once been the Supply Depot.

She struggled to her feet. "I thought we were going to Base Two."

His strides took him rapidly away from her.

The exoskeleton strengthened her trembling legs, but the mud sucked her back, weakening her. "Logen!"

He saw her struggle without the hover disk. His jaw tightened. He returned to her side and offered his massive shoulder, helping her to hobble over the terrain.

"What are we doing?" she asked, over her strain.

"We're going to hunker in close to the depot and fight."

"We don't have the weapons to make a stand."

Grimness darkened his voice. "I'm not going into that jungle with you. We'll fight here with whatever we find left."

They reached the edge of the foliage surrounding the billowing smoke.

A hover bubble whirred off to their right.

Logen pushed them both to the ground. The hover bubble whirred nearby, then farther away, circling the smoldering depot building. Logen crawled forward on his belly and peered through the fronds.

"Who is it?" she whispered.

"They're behind the smoke."

A shockingly familiar whine sliced through the air and slammed into the smoking depot.

She clapped her hands over her ears. Logen dropped

flat and did the same.

A furious explosion rocked the forest. The impact screamed over their backs, roaring. Foliage flattened on top of them, rattling and shredding. Overhead, trees shrieked and groaned and toppled.

Dirt pounded them, falling like a rain of fists on their exposed bodies. One crushing boulder bounced off her exoskeleton and dented the metal into her hip.

When she finally had the strength to look up, she saw nothing.

The Supply Depot had been turned into a crater.

Someone had shot the depot with a cliff-breaker missile.

Another hover bubble whirred through the smoke and set down. Red laser targets played against the smoke.

Infrared.

Logen gathered her up and raced back into the jungle. She didn't ask him where they were going now.

They ran.

The sober afternoon passed into night.

Logen led the trek, whacking through vegetation with his knife, and Talia held onto his shoulder, struggling to move in her damaged exoskeleton. She had to rest often, and discouragement made her exhausted and depressed.

He knew the feeling.

"Maybe the androids think we're dead," she finally said, with a groan, resting on a hill beside a pit of ooze.

"Maybe so."

"We could stop here."

He carved the last shard off his new spear and slid his knife back into its holster. "You ready?"

She scowled.

"I could carry you."

Now he'd pissed her off. She snarled. "You can't carry me. You'll have another 'physiological reaction.'"

She really hated that term.

"I'll work it out," he said dryly.

"You can't carry me and your weapon. What's that, a prison shiv?"

He shifted his spear. "It's not a shiv."

"I've seen better spears in children's books. It's a shiv."

"I was only 'in prison' for one day. Not exactly enough time to learn how to make a shiv."

She blinked.

He tested the weight and balance. Hopefully it was sharp enough to drive between the segmented carapace of a growling black centipede. Several had reared up and waved menacingly along the path.

She had gone silent.

He turned to check on her. Keeping her in his peripheral, always.

She had a funny expression on her face. "You went to prison for killing your team member for one day?"

Ah. The error appeared to him. He waved it away and tapped his stents. "Long enough."

"They must have hated the guy."

"Daylight's leaving. Let's go."

"One day in prison and you still got those?" Her scowl rose to his stents. "Can you, you know, tell anything from those?"

Old warnings fought to keep him silent. Safer not to tell anyone. Safer not to speak at all about his malfunction.

But she was glaring as if they had to be good for something.

He tilted his head one way, then the other. Risking the truth. "Magnetic north is that way."

"You can't pick up robot broadcasts or anything?"

"That would make it too easy."

Her scowl turned thoughtful, then a little fearful. She looked away.

Fuck.

She'd looked away fearfully like that a few times since

he'd lost his temper in the Supply Depot. Did she know he'd been about to confess his feelings despite his promise, and it frightened her?

"Come on." He tapped the end of the spear against the crusty hill.

A strange scratching sounded under their feet. They both paused and listened. Seconds later, the scab shifted beneath Talia and fist-sized black centipedes erupted from the hill.

She struggled to rise. "Dammit."

"Time to go," he said, scooping her up.

The small centipedes reared up, emitted squeals, and hurtled black pitch. They scraped off insects and ran deeper into hell.

They descended into unmapped primordial jungle. An odd heaviness pressed on them. Misty ghosts materialized between the thick, black trunks.

Darkness fell like a blindfold, and they were forced to stop after fleeing only a short distance from the Supply Depot.

Talia spotted a broken off tree high above android-levels where they could hide for the night.

Logen tested the slippery black vines hanging down. They oozed from his grip like eels. He gripped harder.

Talia rested the exoskeleton at the base of the tree and he helped her up to a crotch wide enough for both of them to wedge in.

She selected a branch.

He pulled her back and tugged her into his arms.

"Hey," she protested.

He curled protectively around her like a shell, his back against the tree, her seated firmly in his lap. Nothing was touching a hair on her body without going over him first.

"This isn't going to be comfortable," she warned.

Fuck comfort. Nothing felt as good as her in his arms anyway.

"Do you want first watch or should I?"

"Relax."

"Logen, one of us has to set a watch."

"You need sleep."

"So do you."

"I'm not losing you again."

Slowly, by degrees, she relaxed and nestled into his arms, where he most needed her to be. The darkness descended to absolute pitch. She sucked in a breath.

He tightened his grip. "Sleep if you can."

New strange noises hissed and skittered overhead. Tentative feelers tugged at his exposure suit, and invisible creatures wriggled across his arms and legs and shaved head. He picked them off before they got to Talia. This was another crap night in the mercenaries.

Except Talia nestled in his arms. Her hot body squeezed against his. Her ass was cupped by his lap, and if she moved at all, she was going to stroke it against his hardening cock. Her breasts rested against his taut forearm, and he palmed her waist. He could rest his chin on her head. One of her soft hands idly stroked his forearm, tracing lines on him.

It was the best night of his life, also hands down.

She added to it. "Logen, tell me a bedtime story."

Sexy images thrummed through his head. "Like what?"

Her next words wrecked it like pouring ice water over his body.

"Like what happened that night."

Shit. "That night?"

"When I died."

"We went to Base Two to pack up." His voice cracked. He cleared it. "It was an ordinary assignment. Normal."

"We didn't talk or do anything?"

"Nothing out of the ordinary."

She didn't say anything for a long minute.

His heart started to return to normal pace.

Then, her voice turned to a whisper. "Logen, I'm afraid."

Double shit. "Of me?"

She turned her head to his stents. So deep in the jungle, no moon was visible; he couldn't see anything, not even the whites of her eyes.

"Should I be?"

"No."

She turned away again. "Then no. I'm afraid of *me*."

The ice melted. He squeezed her. "We'll get your restore point remade. Don't worry."

"That, sure. But what I'm really afraid of is my old life. My civilian life. The feelings from back then have started leaking through."

He knew what that was like. It had started happening almost the moment he met her.

Want. Hunger. Need.

"It's terrifying."

"Right?" She straightened again, accidentally grinding her sweet ass right into his quivering cock. "I was weak, frightened if someone raised their voice in a restaurant. I was irresponsible, always waiting for someone else to save me. I let a worthless guy push me around."

His hackles started to rise.

She snorted as she settled back. "Now I spar with men twice my size. And I beat their faces in. Why should I feel anything like what I felt back then? I'm not the same person."

"You just got resurrected," he said, ignoring the tug of fear in his gut at how this would be her last until they re-encoded her restore point. "You get a pass."

"Yeah." She stroked his arm. "The other similarity to back when I was a weak, irresponsible, whiny civilian, is that I was also happy."

He let the silence lengthen between them.

Was she saying that, despite everything, she was happy right now?

"I'm jealous of you and Daz." She traced his wrist bone, sensuous and circular. "I left behind a baby brother.

114

He's over a hundred now." Her voice saddened. "I missed his whole childhood."

"You going to see him when you get out?"

"First thing." She rested her head on his shoulder. "I hope he turned out okay."

He breathed in her feminine scent. Like vanilla and whiskey, vulnerable and fiery-bright. And intoxicating.

"How about you?" she asked. "What's the first thing you'll do when you get out?"

"Not go home, that's for damned sure."

"Why not?"

"People from happy families wouldn't understand."

"My parents divorced the year after my brother was born," she said simply. "When I tried to escape from Rezo, my mom wouldn't let me stay with her because she was entertaining clients for her new business, and my dad told me if the guy was such good friends with the local authorities, I should try harder to make my own friends."

He didn't realize, but his hands had automatically formed fists.

"Dad regretted it, I guess, but then it was too late. My brother," she switched back to the happiness, "was the best thing that ever happened to me. I got to be like his mom, even though I was way too young for the responsibility."

"How old were you?"

She calculated. "Three decades? Four? Too young, that's for sure."

He shared her laugh. Everyone knew not to have children until they were at least two or three centuries old. Younger parents didn't have the experience or the patience.

"But it was great," she said finally, laughter subsiding. "He was the light in my life. We had no one else, but we always had each other."

"Daz is only a decade older," he said, too easily telling her about his civilian past despite his intention never to tell anyone. "He did the same for me."

"Your parents split?"

"It's supposed to be illegal. Who saves up the ridiculous amount to have a kid only to break the parenting contract?"

"Mine didn't have one," she said.

"You have to on Saudade."

"On Abrio, you just have to save up enough."

"They're supposed to stay together until the kid's in his second decade to avoid lasting neurological damage."

"Yeah," she sighed and rested against him, "I probably got messed up some after the second decade."

"It fucking sucks. I'd never do that to my kids."

"Of course you wouldn't," she said. "You'll be a great father."

His heart swelled. She might as well have reached right into his heart and squeezed. His chest seemed too small to contain his organs, because they were pounding to awareness of Talia.

She didn't compliment people. She spoke the truth as she saw it.

His spotter.

"So what happened?" she asked. "In your family."

He swallowed the lump in his throat. "You want to hear that?"

"It's why I asked."

He cleared his throat. "My mom left us for some gig off-planet and never came back. I heard she married someone else and had another whole family."

"Shit," she said.

He agreed. "She didn't care about us. It destroyed my dad."

His dad went to work same as always, day in and day out. But in all of Logen's memories, he never spoke, never looked at them, never acknowledged they were there. He unpacked his brown bag of liquor and sat on the ripped sofa and watched a holo, bottle in hand.

Daz handled their early independence fine, but Logen tried to get his dad to look away from the holo and see *him*. His earliest memory was finding a sharp knife in the kitchen, deliberately cutting himself, and carrying the bloody hand to his father. His father looked through him. As if he were air.

"Daz patched up all my idiocies," he said, skirting the biggest sacrifice Daz had made for him. "To this day, he's always patching me up."

"Lucky."

"Yeah. That's why I don't care if you want to trade payouts. My brother's already with me all the time."

"You should probably check with him before giving away his freedom card." She rested her hand on his forearm and said the words that changed everything. "But thanks, Logen. You're a good man."

Logen stilled.

Talia continued to tease her fingers over his knobby wrist. "Take care of yourself. If you die now, rescuing me, on the last mission before you pay out, I will never forgive myself."

His voice rumbled in his chest. "I'm not good."

"You have to get out. You actually have a chance. And you're so competent and deserving and good—"

"I'm *not* good."

"Yes, you are."

He shook his head, laughing sardonically. "No."

"You are."

The dangerous rumble sounded in his chest again, and his heart swelled another size too big. "Talia, don't."

"You know the moment I knew?"

He didn't.

"On that doomed escort mission out at the limits of the Nar empire. We were supposed to be watching the president's daughter, who was equally determined to give us the slip."

Out on the far distant colonies, they'd traveled along

117

some barely inhabited areas, especially driving from city to city. And dangling from one of the old bridges, she'd spotted a cart with four barely legal kids.

"I started to call it in, but you jumped out of the motorcade, forcing us to stop, and you rescued those boys. If you hadn't, we were the only ones in the area who had the resources. They could have fallen and died." She squeezed him. "That's when I knew you were a hero."

He remembered. He hadn't realized how in tune he was with her, and then he suddenly found himself on a convoy coming awake from a light doze and staring in the direction she had silently targeted.

Jumping out of the motorcade hadn't been heroic. He'd needed to stop the fear lancing her voice as she called it in.

Shortly after, he'd stopped double-checking her targets.

"The unit leader was so pissed," he said.

"Sirus stood up and took it."

Yeah. He remembered that, too.

"And very good," she said.

That again. The discomfort increased. "Stop."

She took it as a challenge to think of more compliments. "You're a good gunner and a good survivor and a good human being—"

He couldn't take it anymore. He had to shut her up.

Logen put his finger under her chin, lifted, and pressed his mouth to hers.

With their kiss, fireworks exploded in the black night.

Logen's mouth moved against Talia's, fiery hot, drawing her desires to the surface. This time, she gave in and clung to him, murmuring her desires.

"You're so strong," she murmured, between kisses. "So good."

His tongue plunged into her mouth, sweeping away her words, filling her to the brim with sudden, shocking need.

She turned and embraced his broad shoulders, giving her fears and wishes to him for safekeeping. He wrapped his powerful arms around her and crushed her to his muscular chest. Desire burned into her body, flaming into her.

He ripped his mouth from hers long enough to kiss down her jawline to her neck, spreading the flames, igniting the fire. She tipped her head, opening herself to his delicious tongue. He made a noise in the back of his throat, deep and masculine.

She wrapped her hands around his neck and clung.

He tugged her suit collar open, kissing her sensitive neck. Shimmers of need streaked to her center, pounding with a growing ache. She pressed against his narrow waist. The hardening of his masculine strength against her thigh made her weak. He really did want her, undeniably, as much as she wanted him.

He grabbed the edges of her collar and pulled the suit apart.

Her breasts sprang free. She covered them, nervous and hopeful he would like feeling what he had enjoyed in the Supply Depot reflection.

He roughly yanked her to him and palmed the tingling skin. Reassuring her with his body she was beautiful and desirable and he was hungry for what only she could provide.

He dropped his lips to one pointed nipple and put it in his mouth.

Delicious agony squeezed between her legs. She moaned.

He helped her turn and straddle him, writhing closer in the tight space.

She caressed his powerful knee. Every stroke of his tongue drove her to higher ecstasy and every rub of his palm deepened the ache of her need. She shifted on his knee, rocking gently, rubbing herself on every inch of him.

He made the noise again, masculine need.

She arched in his arms. The world tipped backward.

He stilled. Holding her tight, but close, without passion.

She took longer to bring her body back under control of her brain. "What is it?"

"You fell out of the tree."

"What?" She suddenly realized the arching was so easy because she was going with gravity, swinging off the branch ledge and into the unknown darkness.

She laughed and clawed at his suit.

He helped her back into place, wedged against him again, in the safe crook of the tree. "We are nuts."

"You're the nut," she said, letting herself rest her head under his chin, hearing his heartbeat. "But I'll crack you yet."

His chest rumbled. "You already have."

"Good. Wake me for my shift." She started to nod off.

"Talia."

She twitched. "Hmm?"

"Sorry." He stroked her arm gently. "Where I grew up, nobody bailed you out if you made a mistake. They didn't have the strength to care. Then, in the mercenaries, I was in a Hazard Five unit where they wouldn't help their own teammates. Forget civilians."

"Bastards," she said.

He shrugged. "I saved those kids because I saw you wanted to stop the motorcade. You were willing to take on the CO and anybody else who told you not to care. That woke me up. You called me strong, but I think you're the strong one."

Sparkling lights glimmered in her chest. She didn't know what to say.

He held her.

And because it was Logen, she didn't have to say anything at all..

CHAPTER 9

Despite descending deeper into the pit of the deadliest uncharted jungle, moments of beauty struck Talia, bringing out the brilliant sunshine that had taken up residence behind her still-beating heart.

It was because of Logen.

They crawled out of a black swampy goo infested with squishy worms, and then they rested on the edge of a field of sparkling moths and jewel-toned butterflies. Gigantic dinozoids easily capable of crushing them underfoot trudged across the field, releasing the moths and butterflies in brilliant clouds of color. While they sat in the sunshine, resting and pulling squirmy creatures off each other, this terrible situation almost felt like an adventure.

"Tell me we're getting somewhere," she finally begged, on the late afternoon of their fifth day since leaving the Supply Depot. Everything ached, and hunger made her shaky. "Tell me we're at Base Two already."

"We're far from everything," he said, using his knife to cut open the bamboo-like stalks that held potable water and offering one to her. "Maybe two more days. Try to hold on."

She groaned and filled her belly with lukewarm liquid.

"All right? Come on."

The exoskeleton pinched, but it did allow her to walk faster now, almost as fast as Logen's long stride. She used his original spear for a walking stick; he had carved another one for himself to wield. *Don't whine, don't whine, don't whine.*

"Don't become a whiner," he said, reading her mind.

"I know," she snapped. "It's hard when you're so chipper."

He glanced over his shoulder. Surprise shared space with amusement.

"You are," she said. "I'm about ready to murder the entire robot army with newly invented psychic rage powers, and you're just-one-more-mile Mr. Cheerful over there."

He laughed aloud, startled as much by the mirth as by her statement.

It transformed him.

She stopped.

He stopped too, rubbed a hand over his face, testing whether the smile had damaged his unused muscles.

"I feel like I should clap," she said softly. Because a smile on him pierced her heart with happiness. Sunlight exploded outward, a flash of genuine joy matching the warmth in his smile.

"Don't," he said, almost back to normal except for the lingering disbelief. "It's already gone."

"I didn't know you could smile." She stepped forward to take his hands. "You look gorgeous."

He snorted.

"Hot," she insisted. "Smiling is a good look for you. When was the last time?"

He shook his head. Unsure.

"Like I said before," she said, "I've been experiencing more things like I used to. I used to be a chatterbox, and then basic training annihilated my voice. I think I've spoken more since we left Base One than in a century of assignments."

He gentled and rubbed his thumb across her cheek. "Words are coming easier for you."

"It's my old life coming back," she confessed. "It's been a long time since I said anything beyond the yes-sir-no-sirs. Since we both did."

That was because of spending time together. Not in their own rooms, her hating life, counting her money obsessively, planning when she could leave. Now they were constantly in each other's company, pressed together like socks.

He felt the same way. Logen traced her cheek.

She pushed her advantage. "So about those 'physiological reactions'... are you sure that's all it is?"

His expression flipped to wry. Again, it was a new emotion, and she loved experiencing it, even though it caused him to turn away from her with a tossed off comment. "Sooner we get moving, sooner we reach somewhere."

Walking tortured her. "Tell me it's today."

He did roll his eyes this time. "Two days. Keep marching."

Less than an hour after his dire prediction, they ran into the waterfall.

She hobbled into the clearing. Wonderful disbelief filled her lungs with grateful relief, and she laughed aloud in delight. The glistening shimmer of water streamed down into the beautiful lagoon of her memories, more beautiful in daylight. The same old ground rooters snorted and munched rotting vegetables and detritus. Aquapedes surfaced, rippling the pond, and small butterflies flittered through shafts of sunlight.

Logen speared an aquapede and they ate it raw. Health and vitality flowed into her limbs.

She wiped her mouth and tossed the last piece of carapace. She was still ravenous. "Let's cook the next one."

He glanced around. "Here's the fire ring."

The site of their first kiss.

He stood too close behind her. She felt his presence like a shaft of sunlight, burning bright on her skin.

She knelt down in the exoskeleton and sifted her fingers through the ashes for memories. "Feels like last week."

He was looking out over the lagoon, but her words drew his unstoppable gaze. Heat kindled in his eyes.

She bonded to the spot.

He reached out. Every muscle in his arm flexed in a perfect ripple. His wide hand moved to stroke her head. Tremors started in her belly. Physiological reaction or not, framed by the gorgeous waterfall, she wanted to fall into his embrace and—

He retracted his hand, tugging a little. A gross chunk of white insect shit stuck to his hand.

Great. She grabbed her hair. There was crap all over it.

His amusement glinted as he raised a brow and flicked off the sticky crap. "Hit the showers?"

"Me first!" She headed to the waterfall, stripping off her suit. "Stick to the shallows. We don't have scanners."

He snorted. She didn't have to caution him twice. He headed off downstream.

While she picked the shit from her hair and scooped up sparkling green water to wash it off, she tried not to think about his gorgeous flexing abs and the muscles she had felt, and would love to get another good eyeful. She hadn't seen him naked since the Supply Depot.

Maybe, if she hurried to finish up, she could sneak up and surprise him.

A fat, old ground rooter waddled out of the underbrush.

Rooters never attacked anything. They were built to run from the snakezoids, their natural predator, and recycle everything they found on the ground. The biologists had never witnessed a dominance fight, although several rooters had almost fought each other over a particular piece of tasty garbage.

She cinched her exoskeleton and gave it a wide berth anyway.

Its bag-like gut was the size of a storage locker. Harmless or not, alien fauna weren't too safe. It could change its habits in response to foreigners.

Ah, there was Logen. Shirtless, he turned away from her, visible through the brush. His well-muscled torso—

The ground rooter cut in front and turned to face her. Tiny eye spots reflected the sun.

She stopped short. "Don't try it."

Her spear was uselessly far, over by the fire pit. Logen's rested against a nearby tree. Logen had disappeared below the rise to wash off. The rooter stood between her and Logen's spear.

Its nose-antennae twitched as it snuffled up to her boots. It was going to let her pass.

She took a few careful steps past it, on the uneven rocks at the edge of the stream, and it let her go by. She relaxed and lengthened her stride.

The rooter smacked her on the backs of the knees.

Her exoskeleton folded. She went down. Her elbows broke her fall, shooting pain up her funny bone. She gasped.

The rooter's hard plate scooped her boots. Its maw opened to reveal a slimy black pit lined by hard, white molars.

Fear sliced through her pain. She rolled away. "Log—"

Molars crunched her shoulder. A rope-like tongue wrapped around her legs and yanked her into the distending belly. Slippery goo made it impossible to grab on.

The tongue yanked her to the inner cloaca. Her boots went through and touched sizzling stomach acid. Her exoskeleton weakened and started to disintegrate.

Her boots rested on a disintegrating mass of garbage in the rooter's gut.

She was not being eaten by a goddamned mobile trash compactor.

Talia stood on the garbage, hooked her hands around the gums, and yanked herself half out. "Logen!"

The rooter snapped her, raising welts in its bruising grip. Her head hit shallow rocks and she saw stars. The animal scooped her up and consumed her stunned, unresisting body.

And then Logen was there.

His bare fists landed like hammers, his legs flexing like pistons. One blow jabbed its sensitive eye spot.

It dropped its jaw, stunned.

She scrambled out of its mouth, got her slimy feet under her, and pushed herself up to run.

The rooter whipped around and butted Logen's back legs.

Logen fell forward, onto his knees, in the shallows. The beast pushed Logen over and flattened him in the water. He struggled to rise. The beast pushed him deeper, off the shallow ledge and into thigh-deep water. He disappeared beneath the surface. His arms flailed.

The beast stood on his chest.

Talia grabbed Logen's spear and hobbled back, her exoskeleton disintegrating with every step. She aimed for the vulnerable black eye spot and stabbed.

The beast feinted.

She hit the reinforced hide next to her target. The spear bounced away. Its sharpened point snapped off and fell into the water, leaving her with nothing but a wood dowel.

She thrust the dowel into the eye spot.

The rooter ignored her.

Logen's fists disappeared under the waves.

Fuck.

She lost her footing and gripped onto the dowel as she fell.

The dowel struck in the dead center of one beady, black eye spot and the wood splintered.

The rooter scrambled back. It climbed onto the shore.

Logen burst to the surface, coughing and spluttering.

The rooter shook its head. Its tender, vulnerable throat flashed beneath its heavy, armored jaw. It paced back and forth on the land.

She dropped the splinters of Logen's broken spear and raced for the fire ring.

The rooter followed.

Her exoskeleton dropped off. She tripped, landed hard on her knees, and grabbed her spear. She rolled onto her back.

The rooter came at her. The vulnerable weak spot behind its jaw flashed.

She jammed the sharp tip at the jaw and missed.

Fuck!

She was a goddamned spotter. Not a Gun or a Grunt.

The rooter jerked back, squealing. The spear caught the edge of its armored jaw. The rooter freaked out, yanking harder, and forced the spear from her hands.

Oh shit—

It thrashed away, bobbing its head up and down furiously. The dowel lodged in the hard earth. The rooter yanked free, shook its head, and stumbled. The spear buried itself in the rooter's soft, vulnerable throat.

No fucking way.

The old rooter gagged on the impaled spear, coughed, walked in a death spiral, wheezed in agony, and then died.

Talia sat on her butt, staring at the dead creature.

What was that in the grass?

She dislodged her spear and moved aside the skin flaps. Garbage spilled out and, amongst the rock and other indigestibles, she saw a single lavender-purple barrette.

Just like the packet her brother had sent for her last birthday.

No fucking way.

Logen groaned behind her.

She returned to help.

He sat and struggled to catch his breath, but aside from bruises and scratches, and a few tooth marks here and there, he seemed much better.

She cupped his face.

He looked up at her. Communication passed wordlessly between them. He trembled—no, she did. They both did, in shock and relief. His eyes darkened with feeling.

She was an idiot.

Wanting him to tell her about his past, worrying he didn't trust her, worrying she didn't trust him. Everything she needed to know about Logen was already right here, in front of her. His past, his childhood, and his future were nice extras someday she hoped he would share. But her feelings weren't for maybes or memories. Her feelings were for the man.

And the only thing that had held her back was fear.

Not fear of him.

Fear of herself.

But they were out in a deadly jungle, hunted by robots, with no hope of rescue and barely any of survival. Now was not the time for fear or self-doubt. Now was the time to live.

She dragged him against her open-mouthed kiss.

He stilled in shock.

Her tongue found his and she claimed him, all of his unknowable territory, for herself alone.

Several shocks jerked through him, and then he hauled her against him. A warm hum of delicious desire thrummed through her. He crushed her to his chest. And both of them went up in flames.

She straddled his legs, pressing her aching feminine core against his hard masculine arousal. His back splayed, muscles rippling. She dropped her mouth to his taut shoulder and tasted his wet, slick sweat with her teeth.

He groaned, "Talia."

Heart-quaking heat burned in her, streaking from

where her twin hardened nipples strained through the gaping suit fabric against his hard pecs, and the nub of her desire rubbed against him.

She slipped her hands under the belt of his suit and found him.

He stilled.

She reached up and nibbled at his ear. "Logen."

He shuddered.

She gripped the hard, thick shaft in both hands, relishing his tasty hardness and knowing exactly what to do with it. "Help me."

His normally steady voice caught. "What?"

"Give me a distraction." She caught his mouth with a breathless kiss. "I don't care if it's a physiological reaction. I need all of you."

CHAPTER 10

He fucking lost it.

Logen's blood was still pounding from how close he'd come to losing Talia—again.

He'd been right over the ridge and pretended not to see her, because he'd loved the sneaky subversive expression on her naughty face.

If he'd changed and thawed since they struck out into the jungle, she'd gone from an ultra-professional interacting with the world behind shrapnel-embedded glass walls to a full woman who could take care of herself and had enough left over to tease, to laugh, to swear, and to cry. Every piece of herself she revealed was another mark of her trust. He treasured it, loved it, and fantasized about it. Now, she was naughty.

His new favorite.

And then the next thing he knew, she was crying for help, and now they were here. Rooter neutralized by her capable hands, himself half-drowned, and her helping him come back to life in every possible way with her hot little hands wrapped around his bulging cock and her sweet mouth whispering delicious temptations in his ear.

Fucking hell.

"Make me forget everything but you," she begged.

He could do that.

She arched her back. Her suit fell apart to show the creamy undersides of her round breasts.

Logen pushed aside the suit and cupped her.

She took a deep breath, swelling into his palms. Her fingers squeezed his slippery cock. "Yes."

Hell yes.

He dropped his mouth to her pointed red buds, laving them with his tongue and suckling with his mouth. She gasped and moaned. Possessiveness streaked through him. This was his, and so were these. He pushed the suit from her shoulders, revealing creamy skin down to her waist, and owned every gorgeous inch of it, raising her gasps of pleasure with every kiss and caress and squeeze.

She gripped his iron-hard legs with her thighs.

And then she pulled his suit down. His arousal sprang free. Her eyes glowed with hunger and she licked her lips.

Oh, yeah.

He cupped her through the suit. Her hunger glowed and she arched against his palm. And then, while he was working her suit down to reach her nakedness, she ran her little tongue across her hands and gripped his rock-hard cock, squeezing him with her own wetness.

His erection pulsed with pleasure.

Her naughty smile curled. "Feels good?"

He grunted. "Feels great."

Her smile widened—the right answer, on every level—and she stroked his long shaft. Endless pleasure built up to bursting.

He worked her suit free and gripped her mons.

Her efforts slowed. Her eyes glazed and she closed them, breathing out.

Soft new curls tickled his rough fingers as he found her liquid center. She gasped and canted her hips, urging him on.

He plunged deep into her honey wetness, stroking her

to humming.

And then she gripped him with renewed energy and stroked him once, twice, three times. His body clenched. She was hot and bouncing and naked and beautiful, and powerful arousal burned in her furnace cheeks, and she clenched her thighs on him with a back-arching orgasm that squeezed his fingers deep in her and he exploded, striping her and the water and the world with his own incredible release.

She clung to him for a long, long time. Resting her head on his shoulder, her fingers loosened around the still-hard root of his shaft. Interconnected. He would hold it for the rest of his fucking life if she asked.

Finally, she pushed back with a sigh. Dark circles from their sleepless nights colored her face, but she still looked disheveled and gorgeous, like a perfect woman. "Guess it's time for a second shower."

This time, they washed together.

He was never letting her out of arm's reach.

They kindled a fire with a starter she found in the rooter's guts; the owner's markings were eaten off by acid, but the starter liquid ignited on contact with air. Then they toasted the rooter using Iren's method and having about the same results. She had a funny look on her face when she started eating the char.

"Not bad," he commented. "Better than raw aquapede."

"It feels cannibalistic."

He raised a brow. The thing had tried to eat her, which proved biologists didn't know as much as they liked to pretend.

She sighed and handed him a woman's chronometer.

"It got into someone's gear," he guessed. "When we were here last."

"Mine," she said. "And it wasn't in my gear. It was on my wrist."

"This thing ate you?" He kicked the half-cooked hind.

"Probably after I was already dead." She squinted at the meat.

Well. He'd kill it all over again if he could.

He bit into it more viciously than necessary. "Tastes delicious."

She smiled wanly. "You said we're two days from Base Two? The creatures don't roam far. Any chance I took the hover bubble and came here myself?"

"Why?"

"Could it have been because of something you said?"

The night stilled. The fire popped and sparks floated up on heat waves into the clear night sky.

Persistence. That was Talia. When she realized he was double-checking her spots, she triple-checked them. When he paused an operation to rescue civilians, she called in backup to get them out of harm's way. Why did he think she was going to give up on this detail, just because he wished it never happened?

He felt his head shaking, denying it had ever happened, even as he broke down and told her what fucking idiocy had gone down. "We were talking about us."

"That night, right before I got murdered?"

"Yeah." He shook his head. So fucking stupid. "I thought maybe you'd want to... ah..."

"Continue what we started here all those weeks ago?" she suggested. Her warming gaze both helped and made the whole confession infinitely harder to choke out. "Because we were stationed alone together for the whole night like so?"

"Yeah."

She continued to stare at him.

"And if, you know, you wanted to make it more official and apply for joint bunks or some shit." It came out in a rush. Whew. Fucking done.

Her expression flattened. Just like that night.

He waited a second.

A very long second.

"Wow," she said. "I just never... wow. Huh."

Not, *Wow, she was thrilled* this time. Not *wow, we've been through so much and I can't live without you*, or she realized how much she really did like him, or she wanted to make it official after all.

Just, *Wow.* And a slightly confused, *Huh.*

He scrubbed his face, unwilling to see the same goddamned conversation play out all over again. "It was just an idea."

"No, I get that. I don't really... huh."

Fuck.

"Right, so, yeah. You don't have to worry about any misunderstandings from this afternoon. We're both isolated and under stress. It happens, like a physiological reaction."

Again, silence thinned the veil between their crackling fire and the infinite universe overhead encompassing space.

She blinked as it all finally clicked. "*I* called it a physiological reaction to stress. And then I turned you down."

"You remember?"

"No."

Right. No, she'd died only a few hours later, so of course those memories had died with her and not been part of the ones she'd saved in her last restore point.

"I'm so sorry." Sympathy was always her first stop. "Really, Logen."

He couldn't look at her.

Bunking together wasn't like contracting with the mercenaries. It wasn't like marriage. Hell, it wasn't even that permanent of an arrangement. And she still said no.

They were both enslaved by a corporation that could reassign one of them into a different unit without any care about their official bunk status. Or Talia could promote out of Hazard Zero as soon as she racked up enough performance credits, leaving him behind.

She had easy outs and she still didn't want to share his bunk.

Talia squeezed his knee. "It's not you. It was all me."

The pieces of shrapnel embedded in his heart after her original denial wiggled free and coursed like hot lead through his bloodstream. "You said the same thing that night too."

"Yeah, I probably did. But I—"

"It's okay," he interrupted. "I don't want to anymore either."

Her tone dropped. "You don't?"

He shook his head. His heart cracked in half and the damned stents did nothing. "It's better not to change things from how they used to be. Safer for everybody."

"Right." Her smile seemed sad. "Well, we're not any closer to figuring out why I came out here."

So apparently the conversation was over.

The shrapnel embedded into his veins, squeezing pain with every single beat of his heart. He spoke, hardly understanding what he said. "And who returned your hover bubble and restored the force shield."

They took turns on watch. The fire frightened off all predators and the clear night lasted until almost dawn. Clouds moved in and drizzled.

She poked around the gory slime in the carcass and returned with an incredible find: a small piece of metal. "My badge comm. Let's see if it saved the last recordings."

He packaged up the overnight-smoked rooter meat while she scraped off the accumulated chemical scaling and cleaned the controls. By the time the drizzle had increased to a fire-dousing spatter, she had it operating.

"There is something." She stood in the pouring wetness, held up the badge, and pressed play.

"...ssss...about our Logen. It's...sss...important. Meet...sss...waterfall? Sss..."

A cold, hard ball formed in his stomach.

"I don't recognize the voice," Talia was saying, as she

pocketed the badge comm for later. "It could be male or female. The player is too warped. Can you tell who it is?"

He shook his head slowly. "Too distorted."

But the truth was clear.

It wasn't a biologist they'd recently met. It wasn't someone in Bad Company who barely cared. None of them would dare call him "our Logen."

The person who lured her out and murdered her was someone on their own fucking team.

Lightning cracked across the blackening morning sky and storm winds shook the trees. He finished packing up in the drenching downpour. A second later, thunder boomed.

Not only thunder.

Dark clouds coated the sky, and no lights marked the ship. Low engines swept over their region.

They raced under the furious waving trees. Last night had been so clear. Clear enough, perhaps, for a satellite image of their fire.

"I don't know who to hope is up there," she said, soft.

He touched her, shoulder to her back. She glanced up at him, a soaked profile in the stormy darkness.

The noise faded.

Then it returned.

Along with turret gunfire. The lagoon bubbled with ammo and chewed up the ground, erupting dirt in the iconic pattern of an atmosphere-grade shuttle's defensive cannons.

They raced into the jungle, Logen half-carrying her and their supplies, slipping and sliding into a world on fire with lightning and booming with distant weapons fire. Trees swung crazily overhead, dislodging entire ecosystems of branches and collapsing like ancient ruins.

They ran until they had no breath and the firefight disappeared into the distance.

"What the hell?" Logen demanded, angry enough to shout at the storming sky. "Who's doing this? Why?"

"The Robotics Faction," Talia gasped.

"What are they still doing here? Why don't they think we're dead?"

"Maybe we tripped something. Or it might not be about us. They could be using this planet as a base to take over the solar system."

"Crazy bastards."

"Now they know we're alive, they also have to know we're heading to Base Two. We're being driven into a trap."

He turned grim in the stormy darkness. "Then we'll have to spring it so hard it slams back in their cold metal faces."

CHAPTER 11

As the storm grew in intensity, they trekked into a new nightmare.

Trees swayed and fell all around them, crashing into the ground and exploding like a thousand cliff-breakers.

They fumbled through mudslides turned to cliffs, trickles turned to rivers, and trees flattening or exposing their location to the mysterious ship patrolling overhead.

With her exoskeleton destroyed by the rooter's gut acid, she had no choice but to fumble on, slowing Logen down, while the storm engulfed them in noise and fury.

The ground sprouted rivers and they slid down muck slicks into swampy pits teeming with dinozoids in a frenzy feeding on the different insects and land creatures thrown into their maw by the storm.

One descended on her with a growl. Furiously snapping teeth closed on her face.

Logen shoved the dinozoid back, into the muck. It came at him again. He unsheathed his knife and buried the blade in its thick, black hide.

The creature turned away, waddling for easier prey. It took Logen's knife with it.

He swore as it disappeared into the frenzy.

She struggled out of the chest-high mud. "Logen!"

He gave up his pursuit and pulled her out.

They spent a wet, cold night in a rocky hollow above the land slides. In the morning, the crack of ship-to-ship turret fire awakened them.

Someone was coming in fast and low. It flashed overhead, shaking the still-dripping trees.

And something came after it, gunning with the regular kapow-pow-pow of a shuttle-mounted deterrent. It flashed overhead too.

In the distance, something fell from the sky, gray and screaming, a payload with a specific target.

It headed for Base Two.

But it didn't explode on landing.

"What do you think?" she asked.

He grunted.

Yeah. It didn't really matter. "Let's keep an eye out."

They continued on.

Base Two was a mirror of Base One in all the important ways but one. The force shield had been packed away weeks ago, a day after her and Logen's ill-fated night out.

Midmorning, Talia stumbled over a particularly large rock and smacked into Logen.

He steadied her. "Okay?"

"I ran into this." She kicked the rock. It was embedded deep in the mud, under vines blooming with beautiful starry flowers.

He turned away.

The flowers obscured something printed on the rock.

It was the biologists' expedition logo.

"Um, Logen?"

He was already following the rock into the dense foliage, moving thorny palms and shivering vines out of the way to uncover a man-made structure. The wall of the armory emerged from the gloom, glistening with tiny moss, waving worms, and lichens.

"Welcome to Base Two," he said grimly.

"Holy shit," she breathed. "How long was I out again?"

Foliage grew up and over the lips of the main tents; tendrils reached in windows, and one tree burst Medical's steel-reinforced roof as it reached for the tiny bit of sky in the otherwise impenetrable canopy.

The jungle was visibly swallowing the base.

"Don't we still have supplies here?" she asked, as they slipped and slid over the jungle floor into what had so recently been a human settlement.

"Yeah," Logen murmured. "We did."

"They'll be eaten by the time the clean-up crew gets here."

They straddled a log and forded a stream—half water, half insects—and reached the center of the base.

In the center was a new crater. It was from the payload someone friendly had dropped a few hours earlier while taking turret fire from their enemies.

Upside down in the crater rested their Mobile Command Unit, also known as their tractor.

It had been on the main ship. Someone up there still cared about them!

Six wheels were treaded with rock-breaking metal-tipped rubber. Grooves were optimized for running across water, mud, lava, and plasma. Fifteen moveable segments guaranteed it would never high center or bottom out, and thick radiation-proofed, electrically neutral, reinforced walls embedded with solar flare resistant, expedition-grade polarizing glass protected the inhabitants from extreme temperatures and external danger.

The tractor had its own comm system. It broadcasted farther than the nearest star, as soon as it had a clear line of sight.

"Oh yeah," she breathed, starting toward it with open arms. "We could transmit to the solar station with this—"

Logen's hand planted on her chest and dragged her back, out of sight.

"I know, I know," she said, crouching behind him. Exhaustion was addling her brain.

They approached the tractor slowly and cautiously, searching for anything amiss.

Nothing out of—

No, wait.

Around the other side of the tractor, they found half a dead body stretched across the freshly unearthed dirt in the middle of the crater. The head turned away from them, torso bloodied and scratched with dinozoid claws, and marks where it had been chewed in half.

"Who the fuck is that?" he asked in a low tone.

She shook her head, on guard again. Not a biologist, not a team member.

"Maybe the murderer?" he said.

"It's a recent arrival." Because it was lying on top of the crater. And also, she had played the badge recording, and knew this creature wasn't her killer.

"Maybe dropped from the chase ship."

"That's my guess too." She looked around for the lower half of the body.

Logen cautiously approached.

She stopped him with a hand on the shoulder. "It's a robot."

He froze.

Nothing moved. Nothing at all. Just the distant screech of jungle denizens and last of the storm loosening its grip on the land.

"How do you figure?" he asked at last.

"No blood."

It was too clean. The dirt, still damp from its upheaval, had already started to dry, and it was dry under the loosened bowels of the torso.

"Looks human," he said doubtfully. "I've never seen one so realistic."

She hadn't either, but she knew they existed. "Let's suit up."

He walked close. "It's dead."

"How can you tell?"

He stood over it, way way way too close, and then leaned even closer. "It's not breathing."

"So?" She hissed to stop him from reaching out to check for a heartbeat. Who knew if it had a heart? "Suit up before you get too close."

He acquiesced, returning to the tractor and finding the nearest set of controls. "Ready?"

"Do it," she urged.

Logen activated the righting mechanism.

Pistons pushed out, and the hydraulics hissed. The whole fortress, which had landed on a corner and buried, groaned to its proper orientation. Logen stood next to Talia. She kept one eye on the unmoving robot torso and the other on anything unusual on or around the tractor.

A large snakezoid slid off the slowly righting vehicle. It dropped a half-chewed robot foot and landed on top of her.

Logen yelled, "Talia!"

She stumbled back. Its dagger teeth snapped at her jaw and its poison-tipped claws raked her battered shirt. She struggled under its slippery weight.

It smashed her into the ground, thrashing and shrieking.

Overhead, Logen yanked it off her and threw it. The snakezoid flew into the air, landed on distant vegetation, and undulated away.

She sat on the ground, heart thumping, a moment away from the adrenaline shakes.

Logen stood over her, his head turned to watch the snakezoid, his broad back silhouetted against the cool, white sky.

He looked like her long-ago dream.

A rescuer.

His back rippled with muscles, and she knew exactly what they felt like clenched with his orgasm.

And she had rejected him.

It made so much sense. Damn her earlier self. Of course she had rejected him. Her heart demanded she grab onto her beautiful Gun and never let him go. Logic dictated she reject him for the same reasons she had done so before.

There was no point in falling for a man about to pay out. Or who wouldn't share himself with her. Or who cloaked the important things in lies.

But now she knew him so much better. She needed him like sunshine. The waterfall wasn't enough. She wanted all of him, right now, and for all time.

Talia pushed her musings aside and forced herself to pay attention to their surroundings.

The future only mattered if they made it out of this jungle alive.

She focused.

She put her palms on the ground and shoved herself to her feet. The shakes started, like they always did. In a battle, she took stimulants to get tight focus with diamond precision. In real life, she got the hard chaos of adrenaline.

He enfolded her into his arms.

"I'm fine," she protested.

He squeezed her so hard, stroked her cheek, tucked her head under his chin, and rocked her. "Don't go away from me. Don't go away from me. Don't go away from me."

"I'm not going anywhere," she said softly.

His wide hand spanned her back. He nuzzled her gently for a kiss, confirming her life with his lips. The kindness, the gentleness of his intense passion touched her heart like a glowing shard of fallen starlight.

She looped her arms around his tapered, muscular waist. Skinnier after all these days without enough food, but always and indelibly her Logen.

Beyond their embrace, the fortress finished righting itself with a pleased groan and another satisfied hiss.

When it had rolled off the line, the tractor had been the

top of its class for mobile expedition forces, and had probably gone straight to the top Hazard Five team.

They parted reluctantly to face the next challenge.

Logen gripped the door handle, pulled it out, and turned it.

Nothing happened.

Because this was Hazard Zero. It was a long time since this baby had been the top of the line.

He turned the handle several more times. Sweat glistened on his brow. He started to mutter.

"Try pulling it all the way in the other direction, then try to open it, then all the way back, then try to open it again," she suggested, scratching her neck. "I've also seen Iren tap five times on the pilot's window before trying it. He says you've got to get the attention of the ghost pilots of the past."

He looked at her, his irritated grimace asking the question.

"Who knows?" she said. "I'm telling what I saw."

He wiped his brow, then reached up and tapped the window over his head, looking at her.

"Try it," she said.

He twisted the handle. With a smooth hiss giving absolutely no indication of the trouble it had caused them, the door swung outward.

They walked up the ramp into the tractor.

First, they cycled pressure in the vestibule, even though there wasn't much of a pressure difference and the atmosphere was breathable.

The hangar still held all the shit they'd piled into it from their last missions. Since Hazard Zero skipped from job to job without returning to a solar station for refitting, this was the usual state of operations.

Today, the chaos filled her with teary-eyed joy.

She touched familiar go packs and emergency stocks. Everything a person needed to survive.

Well, maybe not everything. Two bites into a meal bar

washed down with their delicious stored water, she realized what the distracting almost-itch was. Snakezoid poison leeched into her skin and festered, hot and red beneath her fingers.

Perfect marks punctured her skin and didn't hurt at all.

Meaning the poison had already killed her nerve endings.

Shit.

She finished her bar, opened another one, and scratched the numb slashes. "What meds do we have on board?"

Logen glanced back, ducking his head automatically beneath the lower beams of the segments, his own mouth full of the first of several days' worth of missed meals. "Huh?"

She showed him the punctures.

He swallowed and stared for a long, hard moment.

Then, his brows drew together. Terrible flashes of failure and pain crossed his normally calm face. Redness rimmed his dry eyes. He put a hand to his brow like a sudden headache.

She stepped forward, reached up, and cupped his cheeks, caressing the stubble with her thumbs. "Hey. Hey, hey."

He took a slow, deep breath. It held the edge of pain. He took a second one, clean, and opened his eyes to meet hers.

Her heart swelled. "You're fine. Right? I'm fine. We're both—"

A flinch wrinkled his brow and he had to close his eyes again, trying to look away.

She drew him back. "No, we're both fine. This one's treatable. We've got a hundred samples of snakezoid venom and all sorts of metabolized cures. This close to Base, it's definitely one we tagged. Remember when Iren came back with fourteen baby snakezoids still hanging off his forearm? Or the Bad Company guy who didn't tell anybody about his bite for three days, and he swelled up like a balloon? We still fixed him."

He snorted at the memories, then winced.

She stroked the face of the beautiful, kind, incredible man she loved. "What is it?"

"I swore…" He fixed her with his hottest, darkest gaze and she felt a stirring in her belly. "I swore I wouldn't let anything happen to you."

"You haven't," she promised.

"I swore."

"We won't tell Daz." She pressed soothing strokes against his hard masculine frame. "He hates it when I show up in Medical."

Logen snorted again, then sucked in a breath and turned to the tractor.

They only found the basic medical kit. Unsurprising, because they hadn't needed the tractor down here.

"There's probably some antivenins in the base," she said.

He looked out at the dense jungle.

She knew what he was thinking.

His brother and unknown others could still be pinned at Base One. The sooner they drove back, the sooner they could assist in retaking the base. They had originally planned to wire up the Base Two comm tower and call home. Now they had the tractor, they could loft the receiver and call when they passed through a clearing.

But now they had to go in.

The buried Base Two outbuildings sat so quiet and innocent.

Just like the Supply Depot.

They suited him up as if he were headed into combat. For all they knew, he was. Heavy shock absorbing, fireproof, heat-resistant, and electric-neutralizing shielded plates encased every vulnerable part of his body, and a helmet sealed in his air supply. He slung his multi-range rifle over his shoulder.

He looked like a warrior.

She got into her gear too. It was so heavy she also put on strength-assists, a military-grade exoskeleton that would let her leap onto the top of the base building with the lightest hop.

Her helmet's seal didn't quite fit around her growing hair. Logen's didn't fully seal around his stubble.

"Don't crack your faceplate," she warned, following him to the airlock. "I'll cover you."

"You stay in the cab."

Her chest squeezed. "We've stayed together this long. You don't know what's out there."

"That's why only one of us should go."

"The tractor's still booting up. I won't be able to see what's going on or communicate with you inside the buildings."

"You have no restore point."

Dammit.

"What the hell am I going to do if something happens to you?" she demanded.

"It won't."

Double dammit.

"Be careful," she told him, through the impenetrable helmet glass. "Be smart. Don't crack your suit."

He patted her on the head, exited the tractor, and waded out into the warzone.

Watching him walk in alone was agonizing.

She worked furiously to get up some surveillance and angled the solar panels to collect meager sun from the distant, closed canopy.

At least his suit kept him safe from biological threats. A dinozoid would have trouble chewing him now; his suit could withstand incredible crushing damage and, in the worst case, he could blast free from its stomach.

But it was no defense from the kind of assault they had faced in the Supply Depot. Or Base One. Even the tractor would struggle to withstand a cliff-breaker.

147

No.

He wouldn't go down. She would back him up. Both barrels, full tractor.

He disappeared inside the main building.

She stared at it, heart pounding and vision blearing. Listening and watching for any danger.

A few minutes later, he exited via a window, clambered over the thigh-thick vines growing out the main mess windows, and disappeared inside.

Her heart thumped and then she resumed her held-breath agony.

Apparently he was doing a full tour, because a few minutes after that, she saw him at the other end of the mess, disappearing into storage. Had he reached Medical? The way through the halls must be blocked.

The tractor controls beeped. Comms charged, and she was already receiving a signal.

Fantastic.

She hit the controls, expecting to see his suit pop up on the main screen. "Logen?"

The signal crackled and solidified.

Instead of Logen, she saw two of her old team members, Navina and Vi.

Minutes earlier...

The day seemed oddly calm and ordinary as Logen stepped out of the tractor. The inner vestibule sealed behind him, keeping Talia safe. He strode down the ramp and his boots mushed into slippery vines and soft earth.

A grackle of some animal challenged him over his shoulder. The shadow of a deadly bird-lizard flew overhead.

His skin prickled all over with the sensation of a glowing target painted on his chest. And back. And head.

Logen shouldered his multi-range rifle and clambered

into the concrete entrance. Slow, careful, cautious. He passed the stacks of boxes he expected, groaning under palm frond seedlings and standing impervious to boring insects. Everything should have gotten loaded onto the final clean-up shuttles. The robot attack had interrupted their plan.

Was it only a few days since the attack? They'd been lost in this jungle forever.

Until now, Talia remained healthy and alive.

He fucked it up. In the last hour. She had been within arms' reach! He was a fucking fuck up and he always would be.

He passed gaping windows low and fast, ducking to stay below the horizon of storage boxes. One held a machine that could synthesize a new antivenin from her blood sample. Too bad it would take weeks to unpack all the boxes to find it.

A millipede the size of a man's skull screamed on top of a box then dropped down and scurried away.

He wanted to be done with wildlife assignments for a while.

With the shields down this long, he hoped the cleanup team wore heavy duty exposure suits.

Medical was blocked off.

He tried a couple different ways to hit it, exiting the compound and reentering at different locations, but boxes and plants cut him off.

This was taking too fucking long.

Somehow, being back at the base where he had failed her made him so nervous he failed at his basic job.

He checked on the tractor. Sitting there like a fortress. The sight of it and knowing Talia was safe inside put him back on task.

Logen gave up on reaching Medical and started searching for boxes marked as medical supplies. They were scattered throughout the base. If he peeled one open with his laser rifle, he was likely to slice the antivenins in half, and the only thing worse than fucking up protecting Talia would be fucking up curing her.

He would never leave her vulnerable. Especially since now, no restore point would save her life.

A clever murderer would sabotage the restoration machinery so when they tried to make another backup, they killed her instead.

His dark thoughts clenched his gut.

Focus. One thing at a time. Look for Talia's medicine. Worry about the rest of it afterward.

In the back of the mess hall, close to the windows for the back side of the base, he pored through already opened boxes of wildlife sample equipment and netting, tranquilizers and guns. Useful if he wanted to arm himself. Not useful for opening a damned crate.

He turned and something caught his eye out the back window.

Through the canopy was the comm tower.

It was lit.

What the fuck?

He waded to the wall where once had been a commark. They had packed it up on their last trip. The one where everything went to shit.

It was unpacked now.

Shivers ran up the back of his neck. All the hairs rose to a point.

A signal was running through the commark. As he reached for it to get more information, the signal winked out.

Someone was collaborating with the robots. Not him, but someone on their team.

He dropped down to see the wiring. His team did a distinctive job. Iren stripped the shit out of wires while Daz was precise as a surgeon. Navina tied her extra cords in perfect knots, and Vi left tangled cables.

As he knelt and opened the wiring access panel, his atmosphere indicator blinked a warning.

He rested on his heels. The whole base was open. How could his external oxygen supply be low? Made no sense. He tapped the gauge. It beeped and then returned to a cheerful green.

Fucking Hazard Zero equipment.

He set aside the wiring access panel. The part he wanted was, of course, all the way in the back. He got down on the floor, helmet to dusty concrete. His hand outstretched and grasped the secondary access panel's plug.

The plug handle came off in his hand.

He pulled it out. It was a local comm silencer, like the kind they used for privacy and studded around the officers' meeting rooms.

He smashed it.

His suit comm hissed and Talia's face appeared in the upper right quadrant of his helmet. Nice. "Hello, beautiful."

She gasped and leaned forward. "Logen?"

"Yep." He reached into the wiring access panel again. "Never guess what I found."

"Drop everything and get back here. Someone's coming to pick us up."

Her news was better.

At this point, Sirus was about the only person Logen didn't suspect. Everyone else was a risk to Talia unless he figured out the real murderer.

His fingers brushed the inner access panel. He couldn't quite reach. "When?"

"Get back to the tractor right now."

"That soon?"

"Dammit, Logen, now. The robot torso thing is missing."

Fuck.

He took off his glove, jammed his ragged nails in the groove, yanked the panel, and stared at the wiring. All he needed was one look and...

Talia was screaming and his atmosphere gauge was beeping and a shadow fell across the wall and nothing made sense.

...and the wall got all wavy, like a heat hologram, and faded to black.

Twenty minutes earlier.

"Daz has cleared Base One of the robots," Vi said, briefing Talia on her local situation while Navina worked on another screen. "Therefore, you may remain at Base Two and await our pickup."

No way in hell.

Talia pointed out the facts. "Daz is grounded without a force shield, hover bubble, comm tower, or way off the planet. We have the tractor! We're meeting up with him as soon as Logen gets back."

Vi's lips thinned. "Stay put. That's an order."

"You're crazy. Tell Daz to expect us."

"Talia, you're countermanding me."

"Well, make sense!"

"It is perfectly logical to remain in place and await rescue."

"It's even more logical to combine forces. Which is what I'm going to do it unless you give me a good reason to stay put."

"Driving there is a waste of fuel."

"I said a *good* reason."

Despite the fight, or maybe because of it, she was so glad to see her team. Bruised and banged up, they had survived the robot assault on the resupply drone and all subsequent attacks, and were now heading back to save her too.

No one was able to raise the solar station. As far as the solar station knew, their two companies had simply vanished.

Of course, as far as they knew, the solar station could have been hit first.

Everyone hoped the solar station was still fine. Because if not, it was a hell of a trip to the next one.

Talia could worry about that once her neck was no longer tingling from paralysis. Back to her local situation.

"Did you contact the main ship?" she asked, since the Bad Company CO must have met up with the main ship and stayed in the area to drop the Misfits' tractor.

"Gone now. The CO has to deliver the biologists to complete his assignment."

Fucking company man.

Talia gritted her teeth. Of course he prized the paying biologists over their ragtag team. Her anger grew as the truth smacked her again. Why brave the enemy to drop the tractor if he wasn't going to check on whether anyone made it out alive? He'd act differently if an important Bad Company team member went down.

She wondered if anyone had told him about Chaelee.

"Well, we have to get to the solar station ASAP," Talia said. "This incident is way bigger than the mercenary corps. Way bigger."

"What do you mean? Logen murdered you when his stents stopped working."

"That's not what you thought before."

"It's most probable."

She glared at Vi for the ridiculous suggestion. "What's wrong with you?"

Dark bruises covered her whole forehead, suggesting she had face-planted into something not intended to cradle a human skull. Shock, and her untreated injuries, clearly flattened her emotions and made her sound detached, and nothing like herself.

Vi regarded her obliquely. "Isn't it the truth?"

"Of course not," she snapped. "The Robotics Faction is using this planet as a base to invade the whole solar system."

"How do you figure?"

"The ships from the attack on Seven Stars have reconvened here," she said. "We're the only ones here, and our equipment is old and obsolete, allowing them to break in and kick us in the face before we realized they arrived. They're going to steamroll over the rest of the system the same way."

Rallying at the solar station was the only way anyone could stop them.

"Why this system?"

"Because of the prison planet," she said. "If they can get past the Wardens, they could pick up those stented prisoners and deploy them anywhere. They would have sleeper agents spread throughout the whole universe."

Chaelee said this couldn't be the decisive strike, and she was half right. It was the precursor. The small test. The big one was yet to come, and the whole universe would become the bloody testing environment.

"That's unbelievable," Vi said.

Talia tapped through the tractor's records, looking for something to back up her theory.

And she found it.

"The CO managed to put the last satellite images into this tractor. There." The skies over the arctic swarmed with ships. "I see troop ships. Empty ones, ready to take on soldiers. This is proof!"

Vi raised a brow. "There are other possible explanations."

"Fine. I'm a spotter, not logistics. Ask Navina."

Navina did not look up from her other task. Whatever absorbed her took all her concentration, and Vi didn't interrupt.

"Your theory is flawed," Vi said.

But Talia wasn't in the mood to debate. It explained the half of a robot they found. The Bad Company CO broke through Faction defenses long enough to drop the tractor and had been chased off again.

Around this latitude, the dinozoids were too interested in snacking on them, as the half-eaten one proved. Safer for robots up there.

"It is interesting to an untrained mind," Vi said. "Who else have you told?"

"No one." Obviously. "I'm stuck on a planet with no comm. You're the first mercenaries I've been able to reach."

"Of course." Vi looked away calmly. "Actually, we may be able to get someone there sooner to pick you up. One moment while we mark your position."

Her signal cut out. Another face jumped as a new signal garbled the screen, interfering.

Vi was talking.

"Just a sec," Talia said. "There's a problem."

Some sort of signal was attempting to take over theirs to Vi. Talia tried to fix it. It clarified enough to see the new signal's location and sender. She sat back in shock.

It was their long lost CO.

Vi addressed her. "What's going on?"

"I'm receiving another message. From the commander."

His words garbled. She changed the frequencies. The message appeared to be looping, sent on an extremely old technology, a signal almost no one used any more, but which had probably been the main signal in the tractor's heyday.

"Eliminate the message," Vi said. "There is no question of my authority. I have assumed the correct place as Misfits CO. The Bad Company CO is of no importance to you now. He is out of the chain of command. I am your only commander."

"It *is* Misfits' CO," she told Vi. "It's Sirus."

Shock crossed the second's face, and then her cheeks reddened. "After fourteen years, what does that disgraced reprobate have to say?"

Now that sounded more like Vi.

"I think he's on his way here." Talia shunted more power and upped the reception. "Do you see him? Near you?"

Vi shifted her gaze to another screen. "No."

Talia increased power once more. Almost...

"It's a tr—" His transmission garbled. "Ab—. Avoid conta—. Robots, everyone is robots. They are capturing sold—. You can't trust an—"

"He says I can't trust anyone, and everybody's robots and..." Talia trailed off.

Everyone's robots.

"Yes, we neutralized the robot threat in our area," Vi was saying.

Talia was used to mistrust. Turning away from her teammates when she should have relied on them had dropped her down the ranks until she bottomed out in Hazard Zero.

But she *knew* her teammates in the Misfits. She had gotten to know them, despite her inability to trust.

For the first time, Talia saw Vi not as exceptionally calm and calculating in the face of disaster, but inhumanly calm. Her emotions flattened below subzero. She was cold. True cold. Cold as Logen in all of the interview holos.

Cold as someone who had Robotics Faction stents.

"And?" Vi prompted.

"Ah..."

Talia picked out each indicator, or absence of it. A horrible, dark pit opened up in her belly. What was the strange bruising on Vi's skin? Around her temples, right where Logen had his stents. Navina had them too. An identical bruising pattern. And she couldn't see Iren.

No.

No fucking way.

Maybe her team hadn't fought off the Robotics Faction invaders. Maybe they had been captured, forced to surrender, *and converted into robot soldiers for the other side.*

No. She shook her head, refusing to believe her own

eyes. "What happened to your face again?"

"Hmm?" Vi poked the ugly purple center of her bruises without wincing. "A slight injury from repairing the resupply drone. Nothing to worry about."

Talia looked at the woman who had once been someone she worked with, disagreed with, tangled with, and respected. Another person who always had her back. And Navina behind her, always with the oddest humor, had nothing to say. Grief welled up. First Chaelee. Now these two, and also possibly Iren.

Vi addressed her, emotionless because of a stent controlled by evil robots. "Can you identify the location of that rogue transmission?"

Grief could wait.

Talia rested her chin on her hand. "I could. When are you going to get here?"

"What's wrong, Talia? You don't trust something I'm saying."

"I have trust issues. You know that. Don't you, Vi?"

Vi stared. Blank.

Talia stared right back. Goading her.

For the first time in their entire relationship, Vi backed down. "Yes. I do know that. However, you must follow orders."

"Oh. Sure. What possible reason would I have to hesitate?"

"Yes." Vi looked untroubled by her sarcasm. "Remain where you are and do not go to Base One. That will make it easier to find you." She signed off.

Easier to call in an air strike, she meant.

Talia rested her elbows on the console.

Wait. Was that... were those tears burning her eyes?

She rubbed her dry cheeks.

Talia didn't let emotion creep up on her. Not since the incident with Rezo. Emotions weren't safe. She needed to keep her head down and her oculars clear for spotting targets before those targets in turn spotted her team. It was the only way to get out of the mercenaries and back to her real life.

But since the emotions released by her constant contact with Logen, the truth of the suppressed feelings burst through.

She liked her team.

Calculating Vi had steered them through a shit ton of loopholes to keep them together after Sirus took off, and she had their backs against any other ruthless CO. Perfectionist Navina ensured they had what they needed when they needed it, and never let them run out of food or ammo. Iren joked around so they had an excuse to smile again after seeing something that should have run the smiles off their faces for the rest of their lives. And Daz patched them up no matter how stupid their injury, his sarcasm the only poke he administered without anesthesia.

Now they were gone. All gone.

Well, except Daz. He was still alive and in hiding at Base One. And then there was herself and Logen.

Grief could wait.

She had work to do.

Talia tapped the comm to reach Logen. "I know who's behind the attacks."

He didn't respond.

Damn. She double-checked the power and their connection, but he was silent as if his suit comm was off. She couldn't see him in the local area, couldn't get a read on his location.

Fucking Hazard Zero equipment. She knew she shouldn't have let him go alone. Not until the tractor finished powering up and they at least had a chance to check his comm.

Or...

A new thought occurred to her. Vi had spoken to her without any delay. The only people who could speak from far away had a faster-than-light relay on their ships.

That wasn't anyone in Hazard Zero.

But it could be someone speaking from one Robotics Faction-enhanced ship to another, and then beamed down to her tractor.

Meaning all of their signals were potentially unsafe and easy to tap. And trace.

How long had Vi and Navina been under robotic control? Surely not before the resupply drone incident. What about Iren? He seemed too emotional, but then, they all did.

She pulled out her acidified badge and plugged it into the tractor's speakers. The same message played back, scuffed and distorted.

"...ssss...about our Logen. It's...sss...important. Meet...sss...waterfall? Sss..."

She tried audio programs, but all she could get was one additional word.

"...ssss...about our Logen. *It's real important.* Meet...sss...waterfall? Sss..."

It's real important? She played it over and over, trying to pinpoint anything else. Man or woman? Human or robot? She couldn't tell.

It's real important.

That phrase sounded familiar. Someone used it. She couldn't remember who shortened "really" to "real" in normal conversation.

Maybe Logen would know.

Speaking of which, suddenly a scuffed wall appeared on a small screen and Logen's incredible, wonderful, sexy voice crackled over the comm. "Hello, beautiful."

She gasped and leaned forward. About ready to kiss the mic. "Logen?"

"Yep." The screen showed him looking at an open wiring access panel. Never guess what I found."

That could wait. "Drop everything and get back here."

His gloved hand disappeared into the access panel. The wall filled the entire screen. He grunted.

How to get him moving? "Someone's coming to pick

us up."

"When?"

Fucking hell. "Get back to the tractor right now."

"That soon?"

"Dammit, Logen, now."

She booted up the local holos, put on her spotting oculars, and planned their escape route.

They had to get the hell out of there. If the robots were stationed in the arctic, she needed to be out of their strike zone. Any ships could drop by and nuke their location at any time. Or they could release a hundred more androids, or a thousand more, and swarm over the tractor, and burn their way in.

Or they could send another human-like one to trick them...

She glanced out at its last location. Oh no.

"Logen?" She spoke into the mic, dead sober. "The robot torso thing is missing."

Something started beeping.

"Maybe it got eaten," she said, picking through the possibilities as the beeping on his side of the comm got louder, "and maybe it woke up and crawled away. With robots, you never can trust they're actually d—"

Logen collapsed.

CHAPTER 12

What the hell was going on in there?

Talia gripped the controls and shouted at him. "Logen? Logen!"

Logen's vitals tanked. His atmosphere indicator flew off the charts, buried in the red, and a hazard alarm beeped.

Fuck.

His suit cam focused on a blank wall. His outstretched hand went lax and dropped the wires. Where the hell was his glove?

She'd taken her eyes off the screen for an instant to search for that robot torso bastard. It only had arms. It couldn't go that damned far.

Logen's heart beat faster and faster, and the atmosphere levels of his blood dropped lower and lower.

He was suffocating.

In a minute without oxygen, his heart would stop. Then, in four minutes, his brain would start to die.

Stay in the cab.

She had no restore point.

He did have one. He could be resurrected. Surely nobody would put stents in a criminal anymore if it turned them into a slave to another force. She could leave him behind to die with all of the memories of the rooter and the waterfall and the three weeks he took a beating for her and losing her and their first kiss and—

Fucking hell.

She sealed up her armor and grabbed her strength-assists, snapping them on her suit joints as she waited for the pressure seal to let her out of the tractor.

Caution.

She ran across Base Two, the strength-assist exoskeleton making every hobble into a stride of giants, her head aswivel and eyes recording every detail. Where was the goddamned robot torso? Not dangling from the mouth of a hungry dinozoid. She passed the place it had been in the dirt.

Hand prints and drag marks disappeared into the mess hall.

Fuck fuck fuck fuck fuck fuck fucking hell.

Logen's heart rate, projected from her in-helmet speakers, slowed and weakened.

A labyrinth of boxes made the corridor into an ambush zone. It stretched from the entrance to where it disappeared into sinister shadows.

She moved, fast and low. Her oculars analyzed every detail, tracing Logen's passage and the robot torso's. Through zooming lenses, the boxes and foliage and insects looked strange and unfamiliar, both brighter and more frightening, as she entered the cold, calculated warzone.

Something moved in the dark.

She lifted her gun and shot.

A black millipede sliced in half, screaming. Its top half toppled. The bottom collapsed. Her laser smoked black, holing a samples crate.

Fuck.

Now the robot thing would know she was inside. It would know she was armed. It would know she was coming.

Logen's heart stopped.

She tore down the dead-end aisles, reached the window to the back of the mess hall, and backtracked. Where the hell was he? Where—

There he was. Still, on the ground.

Her oculars flipped to highlight the atmosphere. Three flammable tanks of dinozoid tranquilizers hissed next to his body. Dinozoid tranquilizer was heavier than oxygen and the two layers stuck together like oil and water. He was below the water line.

She started for him.

A hand grabbed her helmet.

She spun.

A foreign weight settled onto her back. She kept spinning. Only flashes of color and shadow darted away from the corner of her frantic eyes; oculars picked them out where she would have failed.

An arm reached around her neck and locked her into a choke hold.

Her suit emitted a warning sign. External pressure on the neck plate exceeded critical thresholds. In another few seconds, it would crush her trachea.

There. Her oculars picked out a reflection in the commark screen against the wall. Through her terror, she saw Rezo's shadow strangling her.

Terror gripped her.

No.

Talia leveled her gun over her shoulder and squeezed the trigger.

The laser cut through her attacker, shooting sparks that winked out just before they touched the flammable gas. The robot thing let go of her neck and swung below the laser. She released the trigger before she cut herself.

The robot grabbed her barrel and bent the metal.

She threw it.

Her strength-assists launched the robot across the mess hall and into a wall of boxes, burying him in debris.

She dropped to Logen.

He'd taken off his glove, and his suit had sucked the gas right in.

First step, drain the tranq. Second step, get his heart restarted. Third step, make him breathe in oxygen.

The boxes toppled. A crazed robot, forehead half-melted and face mangled, crawled out of the wreckage and across the floor at them. Sparks spattered like electric blood, dripping inches from the deadly flammable gas.

Correction.

She grabbed Logen, swung his bulk across the concrete like he weighed nothing, and flung him out the back window.

His body sailed out, heavy armor and all.

She ran after him and leapt.

Something caught her ankle and yanked her back inside.

She went down hard, crashing into the cement and smacking her faceplate. A small chip flew off but the seal remained intact.

Behind her, the robot grabbed onto a metal pylon. It yanked her backward. Her suit scraped along the floor.

She tried to roll to face her attacker.

It held her down.

She gasped, frustration weakening her. How could it be so strong? It wasn't a full body.

It dragged her again.

Her metal strength-assists hissed against the concrete, friction rising in the incendiary gas.

The robot grabbed the back of her neck and slammed her face into the ground. Her helmet pinged, protesting around the weakened area. It slammed her again, and a third time. The clear alloy turned white, about to crumble.

Her breath came in short gasps.

She couldn't win against it. She lost her gun. She had nothing.

Rezo—no, the robot—clamped onto her forearm. His

dominant arm wrapped around her neck and squeezed her life out. She arched frantically. Her vision turned black. Her breath left her body. No one would save her. She would finally die.

I think you're the strong one.

Beneath the blackness was a bright burning ball of fury. Rezo was dead.

No legless metal asshole was turning her into a corpse. She was a fucking mercenary now.

The robot let go of the pylon to strangle her with both hands.

She jack-knifed and pounded it into the concrete.

It let go.

She jumped up.

It jumped after her.

She turned midair and kicked its sparking face into the wall commark.

The screen fell in a shatter of sparks into the gas.

The explosion blew her backward out the window.

She landed on the hill next to Logen, cushioned by the gravity assists in the suit so she didn't lose her breath.

Yes.

"I am not dying for you or anyone else today!" she screamed at the exploded robot.

Debris and flaming fireballs spit through the window at them in answer.

She rolled onto her front, flung Logen over her shoulder, and escaped into the dense foliage. Tumbling over vine and shrub, tree root and palm, she dragged him up the back hill, his feet gouging deep tracks in the soft earth.

Behind her, a roar filled her external helmet audios. Flames spread through the whole complex, snaking after them.

He was still vulnerable. His lungs were filled with the gas. If a spark got too close...

No, no, no.

She dragged Logen to the limit of where the jungle cut them off against a cliff, and then she turned back to the exploding base. Flames had already cut her off from the tractor. No choice. She crossed through a river of fire.

Flame licked and heated her metal suit.

Inside the mess hall, pressurized pops of equipment exploded. The roof shuddered and fell in.

At the tractor, she fought with the handle. Open, open, open! The handle turned but nothing happened.

From beyond the wall of fire, something skeletal and shiny dragged itself from the mess hall and crossed the burning dirt.

Open!

She jumped up, tapped the pilot's window five times, and landed heavily with Logen still over her shoulder. She twisted the handle.

The door hissed and swung outward.

She raced up the ramp and into the pressurized vestibule.

The flaming robot followed them. Its face melted off and holes like black pits showed where its eyes had once been. Metal dripped, sizzling, as it crawled up the ramp.

She dumped Logen against the far wall and slammed the controls. Close, close, close!

The vestibule airlock slowly slid shut.

The robot reached out.

The door stopped on its hand. Gears made a grinding sound. Its melting fingers closed in the gap.

She stepped forward, screaming, and kicked it. "Leave us the fuck alone you fucking fuck!"

The robot collapsed into molten pieces, its head rolling back and toppling from its spine, and all the pieces sizzling into hardened screws.

The vestibule airlock sealed.

Yes.

She hunched over, getting back her breath while the firefight continued outside. On her monitor, she suddenly became conscious of Logen's breath and heart rate.

He was alive.

At some point, the gas had drained out of his lungs when he was hung over her shoulder, and his suit's automatic life support had kicked in.

Time to get the fuck out of there.

She twisted.

Logen was staring at her through his faceplate. He looked alive and not happy about it, but the bleakest proud smile touched his lips. "Remind me not to piss you off."

She laughed, her breath ragged in her throat. "You don't need a reminder."

"Heh." He sobered. "I told you not to leave the cab."

She helped him to stand. "I don't take orders very well."

He winced and groaned. "Just my luck. The woman I love is hell on the chain of command."

"You don't know the half of it."

Then his words penetrated her brain.

She paused in the middle of the hangar and looked up at him.

He swallowed, unnaturally red-faced from toxic gas inhalation, but he didn't back down and he didn't ease away.

Rightful tingles raced up to her suddenly pounding heart.

A particularly hard boom rocked the tractor, and he grabbed for a bunk support, looking ready to throw up.

"I'll start the engine."

She left him in the back to throw up while she started the tractor and drove right on out of there.

Logen joined her in the cab for three rough days across a deadly jungle back to Base One.

He listened as Talia told him all about the state of their teammates and their best hope.

"Bad Company also dropped intel about our attackers," she told him, as she patted the tractor dash, "and where they're congregating in the arctic. Vi was right. The androids aren't at Base One any more. They've been picked up."

Made sense.

He grunted. "Picked up and taken to fight elsewhere in the robot war."

"So I assume. If we go here," she pointed to an outcropping near Base One, "we should be able to send a message using the same technology Sirus used to contact us. Get out a warning to the solar station."

"If they're still around."

"Or the one beyond it. Sending the message will make us a target, but it's the only warning we can give. Are you in?"

As if she had to ask.

"Great. We'll get Daz, transmit our message, and go back on the run."

Her face drained of color. She looked as sick from the snakezoid poison as he felt from the toxic gas.

"The Bad Company CO set us up pretty good. This tractor can last forever. We'll give any robots quite the run. Maybe strike back."

Chattering about everything except his confession.

"I forgive the guy for rearranging my face," Logen said.

She darkened. "I don't."

He smiled and tugged the thick felty blanket around his shivering shoulders.

Well, she could avoid his confession all she wanted. He wasn't taking it back. Not this time. He was going to have one moment of true honesty before he died.

He was going to man the fuck up.

"I'm not avoiding you," she finally said, on the third and last day before they were scheduled to reach Base One.

He snorted.

"What?"

He indicated their small, bumpy cab. It was his turn to drive. She could go into the back hangar if she wanted and sleep in a bunk. "There are not a whole lot of places left to go."

"I meant about what you said." She fanned herself.

He was cherry-red and freezing; she was pale blue and overheated. His hands shook on the wheel. Neurotoxins. The effects got worse and worse.

"I don't want you to think I'm saying no," she said.

"Wouldn't be the first time."

"I probably meant I would think about it."

"You said there was no way in hell you'd ever start anything with me, even if I were the last man in the universe, not just the last man on this planet."

"That's a lot of words for old-me."

"You used fewer words," he conceded. "The meaning was there."

She wrinkled her nose and rubbed her forehead. "I'm sure it's because there was no point."

"I'm not the guy for you."

"Hey! There's no guarantee we'll get to spend much time together. One of us could get reassigned and you're paying out."

"That's why we should bunk together now, while we still have the chance."

"That's why we shouldn't, because it will only hurt more when you get ripped away from me."

Sure. Right. Fine.

Whatever she said.

She read his expression. "I told you! I'm sure I still liked you."

"I'm not that likeable."

"You say it so matter-of-factly."

He shrugged. "I don't blame you. It's no surprise a woman like you wouldn't want to stick herself with a guy like me."

"You were paying out!" She smacked her hand on the console. "How could I hold you back when you were on the threshold of becoming free?"

"That's not a problem now."

"Oh sure, we're on the run in an alien jungle *now*." She smacked the console a few more times. "You have to become a free man."

"The only man I want to become is one who's worthy of you."

CHAPTER 13

Talia's pale cheeks flushed and her lips parted.

He wanted to put the tractor in park, sweep her into his arms, and reinforce his message with loving that lifted her to ecstasy and removed all doubt.

But they were less than a day out from Base One, and stopping now could cost more than their lives.

She tore her gaze from his and idly said, "Cliff."

He spun the controls, easing them away from the drop. "Nice, Spot."

"Good reflex, Gun."

Falling back into the familiar patterns as if nothing had changed.

Whatever.

"Besides, you're the one who doesn't want it to be official," she muttered.

Okay, that did it.

He put it in park. The tractor hissed to a stop.

She turned and stared at him with gorgeous, luminous eyes.

"Bunk with me," he said.

A delicate blush rose up on her cheeks. Shimmering tears glimmered at the corners of her eyes. She turned away and put her hand to her mouth. "You have to pay out."

"There's nobody and nothing waiting for me to get out but regrets."

"And why is that?"

His stomach dropped. She wanted to know the truth. She had to know all of him.

"Logen, why?"

Man the fuck up. Quit hiding behind her ignorance. She loves you or she doesn't.

"Because I was a despicable ass who was better off enlisted," he said.

"Nobody's that bad."

"Oh yeah," he disagreed. "Somebody ought to have capped me. Instead, I died of stupidity and ended up here."

"Bullshit."

And then, since she wanted to know more, he told her the sordid tale of how he ended up enlisted.

On the streets, after a lifetime of failures, he hurt people, stole their belongings, and generally made life harder for everyone in the five hundred blocks than it had to be.

"I was on some kind of 'might-makes-right' tear," he explained, as she turned white and green, "because I didn't have anything but might, and I sure as hell never landed on the side of anything right."

A couple of months before the end, he ran into a well-off guy out on a date with his girlfriend. So Logen beat the shit out of him.

"About halfway through, I recognized him from school. He was always kind of nice to me, back when I used to go."

"So you stopped?"

He grimaced.

"No?" Her voice squeaked.

He rubbed his face. "Here was a guy who started out

not much better than me, and he had a girl and a nice jacket, probably a decent job, and most of all, he had hope. He had happiness. Or at least he did, until he ran into me."

She swallowed back her obvious nausea.

Fuck. What did he expect?

He let out the past with a sigh. It was over and done and he had to live with who he had been. His victims deserved no less. If they thought of him every day, he would think of them twice as often. Not much else he could do for atonement.

"I don't expect you to understand," he said. "Hating someone so hard because you want what they have."

"No, no." She waved for him to continue. "I might have been a bitch to the civilian biologists recently. Go on. How did it turn out?"

"I put the guy in the hospital," he said, blowing it right out there. "I might have done more, but Daz ran into me on his way home from work. He had a real job, that guy."

She laughed weakly. "He patch the other guy up?"

"The girlfriend had already called the cops and a medic. Daz hustled me out and patched *me* up, which was more than I deserved." He sighed. "And here I am."

She nodded, then frowned. "Wait. How did you enlist?"

Oh. Yeah.

In comparison to the moment he had realized he was a person who didn't deserve the life his parents had grudgingly gifted him, his actual death barely mattered. He'd been running on suicide mode for months. By the time he actually died, he'd already long pulled the trigger.

"Some girl convinced me to hit up a crime boss's shipment of illegal imports."

"Ah."

"She convinced me to do it on Daz's shift because he wouldn't turn me in."

"Bitch."

He shrugged. "She was right. I pulled the job and Daz

didn't turn me in. But of course the loot was tagged, the boss's heavies caught up to me, everybody died, and Daz followed my body to the enlistment office before he could end up as the final casualty. Lives of two brothers ruined in one," he snapped his fingers, "stupid moment."

She listened. Really listened.

It was kind of a relief to get it all out there. He'd never told anyone the details before.

"So, if I ask you to bunk with me, are you going to say yes?" he asked.

"I will bunk with you if you promise to pay out."

"Deal."

She narrowed her eyes. "Why was that so easy?"

"Because you didn't say anything about me joining up again."

She looked surprised.

"I want to be with the woman I love doing the job I'm good at," he said. "On my terms, fine. I'll stay in until she can get out."

She bit her lip.

"Don't try to chicken-shit out of it."

She smiled, stood, crossed the cab, and cupped his wan cheek. "I am pretty much out of excuses, aren't I?"

"You are."

She rested her forehead against his. "I was thinking it's been a long time since I felt at peace. When you joined, and Sirus was in charge, and we all had our place, the mercenaries were almost an adventure and I wasn't that sad to be a part of it."

No fucking way. "Don't tell me you're thinking of staying in now."

Her smile curved, teasing. "I'm not allowed?"

Unbelievable. She was messing with him.

She laughed, a gorgeous throaty sound, and rose. "All right."

That was his Talia.

She returned to her seat. He restarted the tractor.

Branches flew up against the front, blinding them for a moment, then churned beneath the tractor's wheels. Base One emerged before them, quiet.

He stopped the tractor and put out the solar charging panels. Sensors sought friends and enemies in the wrecked base.

Time to get Daz and then get the fuck out to the outcropping, where they would transmit the attack and their evidence of the Robotics Faction's plans.

As they headed for their armor, a clang echoed through their tractor.

What the fuck?

He turned back to the outside screens.

Daz was pounding on their glass!

Talia had never been so happy to see a blown-up base in her life. The creeping, crawling vines tangling across the downed comm tower wreckage like hungry tentacles were new. So were the pieces of androids strewn around the quiet yard.

And then there was Daz.

He couldn't see in, but there he was, wearing a shock rifle and his combat greens, carefree in the sun, waving and grinning.

Genuine happiness welled up in her heart. Another symptom of the return of her humanity, which she had to blame on Logen.

Logen made a sound deep in his throat. Gratitude.

She had to dash the tears from her eyes as she hit the open button and let his brother in.

Daz stormed up the ramp, cycled through the vestibule, and met them inside. "No fucking way! I'd say you guys made it, but you sure as hell don't look like it!"

He enveloped them both in a hug. They all laughed and talked and cried.

"We have to get out of here." Logen finally ended the

reunion and went to cycle the airlock. "There's an outcropping a few miles away where we can transmit what happened to the solar station—"

"Wait, wait." His older brother stopped him. "The synthesizer's set up and it can't be moved. You need medical attention now."

She and Logen traded looks. The first attack had taken out more trees, and now the fog storm had cleared. They would appear on satellite to the robot invaders.

"You'll be no good to anyone if you're dead," Daz said.

Logen reopened the airlock and they all exited the tractor.

While synthesizing cures for their ailments, Daz told them what he had seen while hiding near the base. The androids were picked up by another robot ship, allowing him to return in safety.

"With a reprocessor and the remains of the armory, I've been fine. Here, med pen." Daz sprayed his brother with dino tranq neutralizers.

"Talia needs it more," Logen protested.

"Soon as her blood analysis is done, it'll start synthesizing antivenins."

The poison in her veins gave her shakes and burning hot flashes. After enduring for all this time, now, in sight of the synthesizer, her tough exterior crumbled. She had to focus on something else not to cry.

"Sirus is coming to pick us up. The robots might be first," Talia said, sharing their communications.

"He always was late to the party." Daz tapped his lip. "Let's load the rest of the medical supplies in case we have to hide out longer than we realize."

They started moving things from Medical out to the tractor.

Daz tried to speak with Talia privately. She paused with him several times, but Logen remained near, and Daz eased off without sharing.

Fuck. Logen had been worse off than her for a long

time. He hadn't been able to keep down food or much water, so he was emaciated and still had fits of cherry-red cheeks. She hoped Daz wasn't going to tell her something bad.

Meanwhile, she struggled with her own illness. After all the movement, the poison took its toll.

She finally collapsed against the old officers' wing. "I'm going to rest."

Logen waited with her.

Another idea burned for her attention. "If anything's still repairable in the officers' ready room, I could use it to play the badge recording."

He raised a brow.

"It's more sensitive than what's in the tractor."

His gaze dropped to the old acid-eaten badge she had pinned to her shredded collar. "Vi and Navina are already stented."

"One of them was compromised before." She eased her headache-filled skull against the wall, warmed by the afternoon, with a groan. "I still want to know who."

He set his shock rifle in the dirt beside her.

"Sure?" She rested her hand on the thick barrel. "You'll probably have to kick out a whole nest of poison geckoes."

"Daz cleared the buildings." He tapped his new uniform lapel badge, making the one she had secured to her collar hiss. "Call if you need me."

She bid him go and closed her eyes.

He loved her. *He loved her.* And he wanted to bunk with her officially.

Which meant he would pay out and then reenlist as a volunteer. The idea drove her crazy. She wanted him out of here, away from the controlling Robotics Faction, and safe. She felt the same drive to protect him that he felt to protect her. That's why she understood.

She had spent her entire enlistment dreaming of the day she left. But how easily could she settle back into civilian life knowing Logen was inside, fighting off an invasion that had stolen their teammates and threatened their humanity, and she wasn't there to spot for him? The answer was that she couldn't. Every day she was outside, she'd crave the security of his touch, and dream of reenlisting.

As soon as he got back, she'd tell him.

Several minutes later, Daz edged up to her. "Where's Logen?"

"Around. Is my antivenin ready?"

"Another couple minutes."

She squinted at his jiggling knee. He had never been a fidgeter before. "Are you nervous about something?"

"Maybe." Daz scratched the back of his head. "Something occurred to me. About you and Logen. Are you close?"

She tilted her head at the protective older brother routine. "Are you concerned?"

"Not really. Logen doesn't have the best track record with women." He glanced sideways at her. "You know?"

"I hope I'm not similar to the woman who ruined his life."

"No, no, no. But you've got a target on your forehead, and if something happens to you, I can't imagine what he'd go through."

Ah, man. Maybe it was the headache, maybe it was the numbness spreading up her jaw to her lips and down her chest to her belly, maybe it was the tremble in her fingers. His question depressed her.

She wanted to be done surviving. She wanted to have made it. She wanted to have won already.

Talia sighed and forced herself to her feet. "Well, I have no plans to kick off, much less to satisfy some braindead metal robots."

"I've got one more question."

She was done with questions, and her groan should have obviously told him so. She turned away from him and saw Logen sauntering down the hall.

"Talia? A question?"

"What?" she snapped, distracted. Did his grim expression mean he had found something or he hadn't? "Is it important?"

"Nah, not real important."

Real important.

The phrase echoed in her head.

It's real important.

All of the hairs on the back of her neck stood up.

Daz's shadow approached hers. The long barrel in his hand pointed at her chest.

She slowly turned.

His sparkling eyes focused on her collar. "Is that acid-stained badge from the gut of a ground rooter?"

No.

He wasn't cold like Vi or ignoring her like Navina. He spoke with a smile. Personality. And his temples were clear. Unbruised, perfect. Not at all like the other stents.

"It was you?" she whispered.

"Sorry, Talia." Daz lifted the barrel. The laser sight stuck on her bare chest.

"You don't have stents," she protested.

"Who knew following your brother for one day to prison, where they didn't let me out of the processing plant, would still result in my getting stents?"

He laughed, a little too high-pitched.

"But it was a blessing in disguise, you see. I was about to fail out of Medical. To heal people, you sometimes have to cut them up, and I didn't have the stomach.

"But then, thanks to the stents, I could eat a four course meal while sopping up a whole platoon! The surgeons were so nice to cover them up with a skin graft, gratis, since I was innocent and all. The volunteer, you know, not regular enlisted. I excelled in Medical and turned into a good little mercenary. Nothing has ever bothered me again!

"Until a month ago, when a little voice wormed into

my brain and disturbed everything." He tsked. The laser target remained on her chest. "That can't happen. I need my brain back so I can stop caring again. You understand."

She shook her head.

"Sure you do," he insisted. "I've seen how you push everyone away who could possibly get under your skin. Friends in other units. Your own team, who's got your back. Logen, who fucking loves you. That's the saddest part of all this. I really do think losing you will shove him back to the most violent, hopeless point in his life."

Daz frowned for a long moment.

Then he shrugged and centered the target again. "Oh well. He'll get over it with his own stents."

She tensed to run.

A shadow burst from the collapsed hallway and attacked Daz.

Without wavering, Daz fired twice.

She dodged.

The shots slugged Logen in the chest.

CHAPTER 14

"No," Talia gasped.

The rifle in Daz's hands pointed at Logen. A strange, dead expression covered his face. And then it lifted and he became Daz again. Shock opened his features.

Logen staggered. His mouth gaped open.

Oh no.

Daz's wail pierced her heart. "No!"

They both converged on Logen.

Blood pooled around Logen's fingers, clasped over his chest. Oh, no.

"No. No. No." Daz's horror matched hers. He stuck pressure tape over the wound, sealing in the blood. "Don't move. How could you do this? You're impossible. You always love too much. And always the wrong people."

Her brain screamed that Daz had shot his own brother. Daz had shot at her, and Logen had taken the blast to save her. Daz was horrified. She was horrified. But Daz had done it, and would do it again.

The whisper of words crossed Logen's lips. "Talia, run."

She backed away.

With the pressure tape in place, and Logen's bleeding

momentarily staunched, the deadness slammed over Daz's face again. He rose. His rifle dropped to Talia's level.

She ran.

Into the base, into the collapsed hall. A dead end. No! There, a place to squeeze through. She scrambled into the main hall that ran the length of the compound.

Flashing in and out of shadow, the ping-zing-zap of a shock rifle missing its target smacked the walls, the barren ground, kicking up dust at her.

Her heart beat in her throat; her blood roared in her ears. Her hands trembled. Run, run, run.

What the hell? What the hell? What the hell?

It had been Daz all along?

She raced past the place Chaelee had died. A black spot marked the ground.

Talia had to get back to the tractor. Get back to the tractor and lock herself in. No matter what Daz did, he couldn't get her in there. She could suit up and save Logen. Logen had to live that long. His wound couldn't be so bad. He'd only been shot in the chest. Twice.

Only.

There, in the mess hall, the emergency comm stolen from the Supply Depot was set up and mapping the pattern of robot ships. One was descending on this base. It would arrive in minutes.

Shit.

She squeezed into a tiny space under a table.

"Talia?" Daz's voice floated, strange and inhuman, down the hallway toward her. "Come out. I need to talk to you."

Her hands fluttered like frightened birds. She clenched them into terrified fists.

His voice grew louder. "Talia, you're not helping. Talia, come out and I won't hurt you."

There. He passed the mess hall.

She poised to run.

Her lapel badge hissed. "Talia?"

Fuck. Her heart slammed into her throat. She squeezed her hand over the local comm.

"Are you hungry for a snack, Talia?" The voice, audible beneath her clenched fingers, also echoed in her ear bones and told her he was returning to the mess hall. He'd heard the hiss from her collar. "You always had a great appetite. It was something my brother appreciated in you."

His boots passed her hiding location. A little dirt kicked up against her still hand.

"You made me shoot him, Talia. I can't lie. That made me a little mad. But you know what's worse?"

His question hung in the empty air, to her right. He could hear her. Tasting the air. Trying to smell her.

"The longer I'm in here, looking for you, the longer it is before I can get outside and save him. You're killing my brother, Talia. Every second. If you kill him on this last mission, right before he pays out, I will never forgive you."

He stepped away. Farther into the mess hall. She let out her breath.

"You don't know what he went through before you," Daz continued, oddly reasonable yet also completely unreal. Like his personality had gotten yanked out, unplugged, leaving only the reasoning shell behind. "He's come a long way. Following his heart, doing what he believes in, having pride. You're stealing that from him, Talia. The longer you make me chase you. Come out."

If he were in the far end of the mess hall, it was possible she could make it out by running. There was a possibility. She tensed for the burst.

He sighed. "Fine."

Her button emitted the call-alarm. It wailed, and his badge also wailed. Of course he heard her. Too late.

She burst.

He was already headed for her and leapt to take her down.

The table he pushed off was damaged from the original attack. It cracked beneath him, causing him to stumble and smash into her rather than catch her.

She dropped and rolled under another table.

He crashed on top of it, struggled up, crashed atop the bench.

She rolled free, darted to her feet, and started to run for the same window she had leapt out with Logen.

Gunfire cut off the route to freedom.

She banked and headed deeper into the base.

More crashes, and then silence. Fuck. That meant he was running.

Her limbs shook.

She darted left down a hall toward the biologists' barracks. A closet with a table barring the door jiggled. The androids? No, a giant dinozoid pushed forth.

She leapt over its back, darted into the next open room, and slid behind the door.

Heart in her throat, she waited, struggling not to breathe, unable to stop oxygen from bursting in and out.

The dinozoid clambered past, six legs moving in segments, into another room.

Daz pounded past her and into the other room. Accidentally following the dino.

She waited until he began banging around in that room—slug-slug-slug of shots—and then she burst out of the bunker room and down the hall again.

Talia turned back to the mess and ran into a stack of flares.

They fell with a clattering ruckus. A booby-trap. He'd put it together so swiftly—he must have done it after she escaped him in the mess hall.

Silence behind her. He'd dealt with the dino.

She turned into the long hall and ran yet deeper. Closed door, closed door, closed door. Damaged by the first blasts, sideways on their hinges.

He started talking to her over the comm badge again. "You're beginning to irritate me, Talia. I need you to die so I can go save Logen. Why won't you die?"

She turned another corner. A dead end, blocked by rubble.

"First, you're killing Logen. Then, you're torturing me. All this time, Talia. I chose to become a med tech so I wouldn't have to kill anyone, and then I realized the ultimate irony, that medics are constantly killing. We're always cutting into the healthy flesh to get to the injury. And then those stents finally gave me peace until that final week, when I was struck with this inescapable feeling in my chest that you. Must. Die. Why is that?"

She ducked into Medical. Nothing in there.

Out the small window, across the wrecked compound, she saw the old office wall and Logen. He was propped against the wall, the shock rifle across his lap. His head bowed. A river of blood pumped down his chest and pooled around his body.

Her local comm hissed. "I didn't want to kill anyone, but you have to die, and you won't stay dead. I didn't want to kill anyone, and then I find myself killing you over and over and over again. It's like a nightmare. It *is* a nightmare. Why can't you make it stop, Talia?"

She grabbed the penknife off the ledge above the bed, cut out her lapel badge, and threw it on the bed.

"If only you would have left that sedative line in a little bit longer." He was in the hall behind her.

Talia retreated behind the cabinet, the penknife lifted to her eye level. *Never bring a knife to a gun fight.* She coiled like a spring.

"I sabotaged your hover bubble and hit you with a cliff-breaker and you got away. I poisoned you and you pulled the med feeding tube out. I lured you to the waterfall and bashed your head in and fed you to a ground rooter, and you came back."

His voice sharpened.

"I've killed you so many times. The crazy builds, a bubbling, gurgling, uncontrollable need to kill you, and it only abates when I kill you, and you won't die. You won't die! Just die, Talia."

His voice reached the door. He eased in, the rifle pointed, slow and careful as an expert Gun. "Come out and die so I can save my little brother. And this time, stay dead."

She held her breath.

He looked down at the cut badge comm. Understanding crossed his features.

She leapt out.

He swung his rifle. It knocked her back. He brought up the barrel.

She fought him, her smaller mass on his, her greater will to survive against his crazy-fueled deadness. He stumbled. She stabbed him in the neck.

He shoved her back, hard, slamming her into the wall.

The penknife stuck from his neck. It did not kill him.

Fuck. Fuck. Fuck.

He leveled the barrel on her. "Stay dead."

Fuck.

She refused. "Don't be such a weak-willed bastard."

His finger hesitated on the trigger. Fighting his inhuman masters. Fighting...

"You're better than this, Daz. You're made of sterner stuff."

...and losing. His expression turned blank as the deadness returned. He lost. The robot masters won.

"Daz was a lazy bastard," he said, robotic. "It's not only his will that's weak."

His fingers started to squeeze the trigger.

She shoved him back, in front of the window.

He pushed her to the floor and lowered the rifle to fire.

Blood erupted from his chest.

One, two, three. Shots sprayed in pulses.

Shock transfixed Daz's face, and then the rifle dropped from nerveless fingers, and electricity paralyzed him as he went down.

She grabbed the rifle away from him.

Outside the window, across the grass, Logen gripped his own rifle. He saw her alive, silhouetted in the window, like a signal.

And then he slumped.

The sound of an incoming shuttle broke through her shock.

One threat neutralized and another appeared?

She carried the rifle from Daz's barely breathing body out to Logen, along with a med unit. He looked at her weakly, barely able to see. "You survived."

"Hold on," she begged, reapplying pressure tape to stop the new bleeding.

"I'm... always ruining... his life..."

"He'd thank you this time. You stopped his controllers from making him do something he'd never want. That wasn't your brother."

"I... killed him..."

"You saved me." She struggled to lift him. "We've got incoming."

"Friendly?"

"We can't be sure."

His bloodless face turned grim. With an inhuman feat of strength, he rose and stumbled blindly with her help into the tractor. She sealed up the tractor and roared the engine.

He slumped against the seat as she drove them, bumping and bucking, into the jungle. "Daz... still in there..."

"There's no time to get him." She drove them under cover.

The shuttle's shadow appeared over the base.

She killed the engine. The shuttle was visible on her external cameras. But under the dense foliage, they shouldn't be visible to the shuttle. She zoomed in as far as the magnification would go.

A door opened and made a ramp to rest on the ground.

Vi, Iren, and Navina strode out.

Logen made a noise.

"Maybe they got free," she whispered.

Logen gripped her hand.

"I'm not going to go check," she assured him, squeezing back.

And it was a good thing she didn't.

In the shifting light, bruises from the forcefully implanted robotic stents still marred their sickly white, expressionless faces. They moved stiffly, unnaturally, without any hint of camaraderie. Behind them, science androids stomped out of the shuttle, wielding guns. With Iren, they swarmed the base. A group returned carrying Daz's body.

He pushed at one of them.

"He's still alive," she said in a low voice.

Logen's breath caught.

They loaded the prone Daz into the shuttle while Vi and Navina set up a missile launcher. After everything was cleared out, the booms of cliff-breakers flattened and then cratered the rest of Base One, utterly destroying it and wiping away all the evidence.

Navina and Vi both looked in the direction of the tractor, following the tracks. Talia tensed. Then, they turned and entered the shuttle after Daz. The shuttle closed up and lifted off.

Leaving behind Iren and a fire team of robots.

He shouldered a missile launcher and started down the tractor tracks. Coming for her!

She started the tractor in a hurry.

He quickened to jogging.

She muscled onto their preexisting track and sped up, leaving him behind. If she could keep ahead of him, then they wouldn't have to engage in a firefight, and she could still reach the outcropping and shoot off the warning.

But when she got to the outcropping and started sending the signal, Logen suddenly slid out of his seat. Blood, hidden by his seat, poured down.

Her hope fell from the sky.

She gasped, shut off the tractor, and cradled him in the cramped cab. He was such a big man. "Why didn't you tell me you were bleeding to death?"

He licked his lips. "Did we get away?"

Five taps sounded against the outside window. Fuck. "Almost."

She hit the locking button, but the red light indicated it was out of service. Fucking shitty Hazard Zero equipment. She scooted up and slammed the inner segments, putting fifteen extra doors between the cab and a relentless, enraged robot-controlled Iren.

Logen's blood pooled around her. "Sorry I didn't get to see Sirus."

The fifteenth door opened.

"You will. He's going to be here any moment. He promised." She ripped open the med kit. No more pressure tape. "You can't die. Don't die."

The fourteenth door opened.

And the thirteenth.

He struggled to breathe. His chest rose and fell, paused, rose and fell. "S'okay."

"It's not okay." She hugged him. "I want to bunk with you. You have to pay out. Okay? Don't die and forget all about it."

Overhead, the sound of another shuttle roared across the sky like thunder. Gigantic ship-side auto-turret cannons ripped up the dirt outside.

The twelfth door opened.

Eleventh.

Tenth.

"...remind me." His smile changed to a chest-sucking cough and he lost the battle.

She hugged his unconscious body while the world ended around them.

No!

She had no gun, the last of her strength was leaving

her, and her vision was fading to black. Still, she positioned herself beside Logen's unconscious body. She would not give in. She would fight to the bitter, bitter end. She was a mercenary.

The hail chimed.

Were the robots calling to gloat? Talia smacked the button. "What the fuck do you want?"

"Well, nice to hear from you too." Her old commander, Sirus, grinned from the comm screen. His salt-and-pepper hair was close-shorn to his scalp and his teeth flashed white under his deep tan.

"Commander!"

"I've mowed down Iren's backup, but I can't get to him inside the tractor. He's very focused on killing you. What do you two have in terms of defending yourself?"

Shit. "Just my brains, sir."

"Good start. And Logen?"

"He's out."

"Okay, well, then. Can you get Iren outside?"

The cab was completely sealed. "I don't see how."

"And you have no weapon?"

"No."

"Okay, you have a choice. Iren's carrying a force baton. If you get it away from him, you can crush his head in. Or, you can throw him outside the tractor with it and I will take care of him with the auto-turrets."

So, killing him.

She gripped the console. "What's plan B?"

"I can try to broadcast a sound to 'drown out' the robots controlling his stents."

Try? "Will it work?"

"We've never tried it over a loudspeaker."

Iren stood outside the final door.

She braced herself. "Tell me what to do."

"Wait until he comes in, then turn the volume up to max and hope for the best."

The cab door opened.

Iren stood blankly on the other side. He had less ability to communicate than Daz. He stared at her without seeing her. His hands went for her neck.

She cranked the volume. "Now!"

The comm made a popping noise and then went silent.

Iren turned away from her to the dash.

"Sirus!" She jumped to guard the controls.

"Shit," Sirus muttered, back to normal volume. "Let me check something. Also, run."

Iren shut off the comm and threw her down.

She hit the deck and rolled. He turned to face her. She staggered to her feet.

He crossed the distance in half a stride.

"Iren, fight—"

His hands wrapped around her throat and squeezed. She choked and clawed at his hands, struggling to fight him off. He was winning.

Her hands closed around something at his waist.

The force baton.

Behind him, the tractor hall gaped. She could crush him. She could run for freedom.

But he was her team.

And she was a fucking mercenary.

She yanked the baton free and smacked him with the blunt, non-functional end.

He grunted and staggered back, loosening his grip on her.

She yanked free, kicked him in the gut so he staggered half out of the cab and put distance between them, flipped the baton around, and activated it. It hummed with warning.

He shook his head and blinked at her. His blank eyes focused. He came toward her again.

She kept the baton between them, and, with her other hand, hit the comm.

A tinny hiss emerged.

"Turn it up!" Sirus cried.

Iren accelerated to attack.

She slammed the volume up full. This hiss escalated to white thunder. Iren was about to slam into her. She crouched to brace for his attack.

His eyes blinked back to normal and he saw her for one panicked, confused moment. "Talia?"

But his momentum carried him into the baton.

The instant his chest touched it, his body lifted into the air. He flew away from her, somersaulted backward, and landed way down the tractor hall. He lay still.

The comm popped again and went silent.

"Dammit." Sirus sounded normal again. "What's happening down there? Who's still alive?"

She swallowed. Ghostly hands constricted her throat. "Sir."

Her commander grinned in relief. "How you doing?"

Everything hurt. "Fine."

"I never doubted you're a survivor. I'll see you in a few."

Talia clenched the force baton. Logen lay at her feet, still breathing. Iren, slumped down the hall, harder to see, but she hadn't crushed his head and he might have only a few broken bones and a concussion.

Her vision flirted with black oblivion as the poison pumped harder through her veins. But she was fine.

She had her team. And she was a survivor.

Logen awoke on a nice bed, in a real bunker, engulfed in the calming scent of well-oiled life support systems. Above his head, five gigantic hunting knives studded a wood bedstead and formed the rack for a collection of guns. Long and short range, full and semi-auto.

Everything was fine.

Talia slept beside him in a barely-there nightgown thing.

Okay, it was more than fine.

He stretched.

She awoke. "Hey."

"Where are we?"

Concern faded her smile. "Do you remember anything?"

If it had to do with how they ended up in bed together and whether he had made the most of it, then no. "Depends."

"We're on Sirus's ship. He destroyed the androids and fixed up Iren."

That, he did not remember. "Daz?"

"Sirus intercepted their ship before he reached us, but he was only able to free Navina. Daz is being taken to prison."

"Why?"

"The Faction concocted some story. They still control the communications."

If he hadn't shot Daz—but he had barely been able to see. Only the silhouette in the window, without his Spot, and hoping to hell he wasn't too late.

"We have to get the word out."

"Vi, Navina, and Iren singlehandedly took over the solar station."

Taking over a thousand-plus station full of the mercenary corps' finest with only three people and Hazard Zero equipment? "If we're going to turn evil, we're going to do evil right."

Her smile shared his sadness. "The survivors were rescued by Bad Company and supported by Sirus, but the station itself is a loss."

"Hell of a time to come back from a vacation."

"His niece was targeted by the Robotics Faction. He's been fighting them secretly for all these years."

"Makes my head hurt."

"Hey, you've been unconscious for over a week." Her concern deepened. "I love you. Do you remember that much?"

Her declaration hit him like a shock. A welcome shock, with tingles. Yeah, that was good.

She'd ignored his confessions before, leaving him uncertain of what to think. This time, there was no doubt.

He took a deep breath. Stretching out his lungs, which were sore, but in the good way of healing and not the bad way of damage.

His silence made her more nervous. She twined her fingers in his hair, stroking his cheek, touching him exactly the way he always wanted. "Don't you remember? You were actually dead for forty-four minutes before Sirus had you hooked up and restarted your heart. Amnesia is possible, but you have to remember. You have to."

Her here like this felt too amazing. "Not sure."

Talia's inner strength returned. Firm. She rolled onto his hard body and straddled his thighs. "I'll remind you."

Yeah.

He shifted, making room for the serious hard-on tightening his cock, pulsing with heat and urgency.

Her bare thighs squeezed his, silken and amazing, and her sheer nightdress floated like a cloud across his hard torso. She smelled clean and sexy and feminine, fiery and smooth as a sip of vanilla vodka. Talia was as hard a soldier as he was, and a much better person. She was also all woman.

"Especially seeing as Sirus knows the truth and you can pay out any time," she settled herself, delicious and gorgeous, "I better enjoy this while I can."

He grabbed her hands. "I'm not paying out."

"Don't sign your life away."

"There's too much for me in the corp," he said. "I'm probably a lifer."

She laughed, her fears turning into genuine amusement. "That's quite the prison sentence."

He shifted, trapped by her silky thighs. "Lock me up and toss the key."

"Well," she leaned closer, "I guess there are things to

save up for."

"Like health and homes and nice things."

"And our kids."

"Yeah." It felt right, saying that. His kids, her kids. "Our kids."

He would love them and keep them safe and always be there for them. Present, a hundred percent, from their wake up cry to their last kiss goodnight. And Talia would be right beside him, fiercely protective and sweetly loving. They would both be kind parents who were also incredibly badass.

Talia breathed out, long and slow. Living in the seriousness of his words. Serious because they were true, and he would keep them.

"Well, at your current rate, it'll only take a couple more centuries to save up for kids." Then, she turned naughty. "You want to practice?"

Fucking hell. "Absolutely."

"Then, there's something you should know."

She leaned over him. Her breath teased his rough cheek; her soft mons pressed against his waist. Her breasts dangled, close enough to palm and caress, tantalizing above his chest.

"I've never been with anyone in this body." Her full lips teased his trembling earlobe. Heat shot directly to his cock, pulsing hard. "Will you be my first?"

He loved her more than anything, and would pleasure her however he could, however she wanted, as much as he could, forever. She was his gorgeous, strong, determined Talia. Way better than him, and yet still willing to give a battered, bedraggled, unworthy soldier a go.

Well, he was working his way up to worthy now. She wouldn't regret her choice. He swore to take care of her for the rest of his life, no matter what.

He gripped her waist, savoring the softness. "Fuck yes."

CHAPTER 15

"Fuck yes," the man she loved told her, his urgent desire a sharp catch in his rough voice.

That was exactly how she felt about her life and their future together.

Fuck yes.

She cupped Logen's rough jaw and kissed him full on the mouth. He tasted like long lost wishes and newly rediscovered possibilities, like the future and the past, like her impossible crush and love returned. He moaned and sucked her in deeper.

Her desire ignited. She braced her hands on his wide, muscular shoulders.

He slid hungry hands up her side to cup her breasts, palming the swelling globes, pearling her nipples between his fingers. Ecstasy shot straight to her sweet, hot, molten core. He knew her desires before she could tell him, tracing the gasps to their source, and lifted his head to taste her sensitive buds through her sheer slip. The hot desire twisted into a wonderful, aching, tight knot. She awoke with throbbing need for the erection pressing against her derriere.

She slid off her sleeping gown and shivered down his

196

well-muscled thighs, delighting in the view of him. He was so wonderfully male, regarding her with a passion-soaked gaze that radiated love.

She traced her fingers along the long, hard shaft of his desire, and encircled the delicate root. Hers. That was how she felt.

He sucked in a breath and rolled her over.

The sheets flew everywhere, and they tangled in a hot, sweet mess that set her to laughing with delight, and stroking the rippling muscles of his wide, bronzed, scarred back.

Resurrected people didn't have scars. You couldn't get scars unless you'd lived long, and Logen was a survivor.

She traced every scar marking Logen's survival, memorizing his body's story.

He returned her kisses and traced her body, lowering to her neck, sweeping his tongue across her bare skin, across her shivering belly, to the aching hot vee between her legs. He licked the inside of her thighs, raising a blistering awareness of shivering need, and then paused, stroking her desire, studying her beauty.

She lifted up on one elbow. "Have you ever done this before, in this body?"

He considered his answer, or maybe he enjoyed the view. "No."

Not that she had a hell of a lot more experience. "Did you want some pointers?"

A half-grin tugged at his mouth. The mirth reached his eyes, warming them. "Sure."

She took a breath to guide him.

He dipped his head and tasted her. Amazing, delicious, incredible sensations poured over her. Intoxicating and satisfying and aching. She writhed with his pleasure. The only pointers she could give were, "More," and, "Yes," and, "Oh, yes," and, "Oh, oh, ohhhh, yes."

He slid in a finger, wet and slick. His broad thumb rubbed her throbbing bud. Pleasure flowed into her body.

His wide palm squeezed her ass, which she didn't know needed to be squeezed, but it felt so fucking good. She dragged his head up and wrapped her thighs around his powerful butt. She needed him right now.

The tip of his arousal pressed against her wet, throbbing entrance. Pleasure lanced her molten core. She tightened her thighs, guiding him in.

He eased in slowly, inch by delicious inch. She stretched around him. Their bodies fit together for the first time. He owned her and she owned him. Their dual identity imprinted on their joined souls.

He blazed at her with love. Fierce, protective love.

Here was the man she loved, buried all the way in her body, connected on the deepest level. Forever and ever.

He tangled his fingers in her hair, same as she had done to him. He kissed her, long and slow. Content, together, for the rest of their lives.

Her body throbbed. Delicious sweetness danced at the edges of her consciousness. She wasn't done yet. She wrapped her legs around the well-muscled thighs and tilted her hips to take him deeper.

He groaned and buried his mouth in her hair. "Talia."

Yes. That was what she wanted.

She chased her pleasure, bucking her hips as he slid in, wet and hot and so masculine. He thrust on her commands. The pleasure built like a rocket lifting off. Delicious sparkles filled her body. He carried her to the edge of the orgasm and it exploded like confetti in her body, glittering goodness, white and holy and wonderful, and she cried out his name. He swore and surged into her, giving in to the hot release. Wrapped in his warm, safe embrace, she let go of consciousness and slept.

Talia woke a hundred years later, or perhaps just twenty minutes, to the summons. The commander was hoping to confirm their course before they took off for the final destination.

Logen was already awake, studying her.

So cold, when no one was looking, he warmed under her gaze to become the beautiful man she loved.

She blinked and yawned sleepily, and then lifted her lips for his welcome kiss.

He brushed his lips against hers.

She felt the soul-tug of rightness. This was, finally, how it was all supposed to be.

They rose and dressed, him easing into his duds stowed in the gear locker at the foot of the tumbledown, repurposed asteroid-fishing trawler, dressing next to her the same as they had done for decades. Maybe his hand brushed hers for a touch of extra kindness, and maybe the gaze in the locker mirror held hers for longer. They had made it, finally, back to the team.

But, down the narrow hall and up the small ladder to the captain's command deck, only Iren and her old boss, Sirus, waited to greet them.

Logen shook hands with the smaller, wiry CO and accepted a back-pat. He asked the same question Talia had asked when they'd been picked up, but with less angst. "Iren. You feeling okay?"

The Grunt had dark circles under his eyes. He flicked a black earplug. "So long as I keep this signal-canceling device in my ear, no problem."

"So where is everybody?"

"Navina paid out," Iren said bluntly, shocking them. "She put in the ear-device-thing, stole our old shuttle, and took off. And Vi elected to go with the robots under their control rather than stay with our team."

"They *left* us?"

"There's more to it." Sirus took over. "Our next project is retrieving Daz. Our spies tell us he's definitely heading for the prison planet. We're not sure if they're hiding him in prison in case he breaks the stents, or if they are using him for a different purpose."

"Such as?" Talia asked.

"Prisoners are stented. As you said, it would be a hell

of an army, and any of us would make a brutal general."

It was hard to imagine lazy, peace-loving, pacifist Daz leading a war. But he was a mercenary. He would never be able to live with himself if he woke up and realized what they had forced him to do.

"We have to save him," Logen said, speaking before she could.

Sirus eyed him hard. "You paid out."

"I don't care. I give it all to Talia."

"Logen—"

Sirus interrupted, "Leaving Talia aside, if you paid out, would you reenlist as a volunteer?"

"I would."

He spoke so swiftly, so truly. But in this case, he spoke for the both of them.

"And Talia can pay out instead," Logen said a second time, emphasizing it.

"Don't be an idiot."

"You have your own good news, Talia." Sirus handed her contract papers.

She held them in her hands with disbelief. "It isn't."

"It is." Sirus grinned. "You can have your old civilian life back. Your brother paid out your contract."

Sunlight burst from her heart, shining in the middle of her chest, bathing her in unspeakable happiness. She hugged the papers. In her imagination, she smelled seaside air and heard her brother's carefree giggle echo through the beachside house.

He had loved her that much.

"We'll miss you," Iren said.

She opened her eyes. Three men regarded her with mixtures of hope and well wishes. Iren smiled painfully, Sirus beamed, and Logen's quiet gaze wrapped her in steady, solid love.

She released the papers. "I'm not going anywhere."

Iren snorted and reached out. "In that case, I've got some place to be."

She snatched them away from him. "Nice try. I'm still paying out. Then," she held Logen's gaze, "I'm going to volunteer."

Logen clasped her hands. "Me too."

Iren gagged. "Can they do that?"

They looked at Sirus.

"Sure." He grinned without having any clear idea, and they all knew it. "No problem."

She hugged Logen.

Then, she pointed at Sirus. "I have to be stationed with Logen at all times, my brother is my beneficiary of any rewards, and I want two months' paid vacation to visit him. No matter what."

"Deal." Sirus shook hands and looked at Logen.

"Same," he said. "And we have to rescue Daz from prison."

"It's our first order of business, now that we have an assembled team." Sirus shook hands with Logen, welcomed them both officially to his team as volunteers, and headed into the battered kitchen area to find a drink to celebrate.

"Are you all nuts?" Iren finally burst out. "You hate the mercenaries! Both of you are miserable, fun-hating assholes. Why would you ever volunteer?"

"I'm a volunteer," Sirus chimed in from behind him.

"You're a crazy old man."

She looked at Logen. "My life is here. And until we get the rest of our team back, it doesn't feel right to leave them."

Before, there was a risk Logen would get reassigned, or she would. Without a contract tying them like he had with Daz, there was no guarantee.

Now they were together. Guaranteed.

"You're nuts," Iren repeated.

"Why so much protest from yet another volunteer?" Sirus asked.

They all stared at Iren.

Iren rubbed his temples with guilt. "I have to get these damned controls out and kick some robot ass."

Logen took a seat at the broken old bench, tugging her down next to him and between his knees. "I'll drink to that."

"Me too," she said.

"Glad to hear it." Sirus cracked open a beer. "Now we're all back. Here's your debriefing."

"That's not regulation," Iren said.

"No fucking shit, newb."

Iren looked like he wasn't sure whether to take offense, seeing as he'd been a member of their group for over a decade and, from his perspective, Sirus was the newcomer.

Sirus poured them all a tumbler of the slithery, yeasty brew, and Iren let the slight go.

"Logen, not only do you have to be stationed together, but you also have to keep Talia with you 24/7," Sirus said, starting the briefing off strong. "She leaves your side for one second, the Robotics Faction can mind control you. I can give you the same device Iren has, but there's always a risk it'll fall out or the Faction will figure out how to circumvent it. She's the only way to keep you safe for certain until we get those completely deactivated and removed."

Logen tugged her closer. "Yes, sir."

"Agreed, sir." She cozied up to her Gun.

This was an assignment they could both commit to. The smile in her old CO's tone as he casually assumed command shared their happiness.

"On to Daz. We can't get to him before he's processed into prison. Our only plan is to break in and bust him out."

Was that even possible? They sat in their seats, considering the problem. Prison planets were constructed to be impervious. A full army couldn't simply break out, much less break in.

And then there were the Wardens.

"What's our backup?" Logen asked.

"Us." He eyed them each soberly. "Us alone. Until our communications go through. We're too far from the rest of the corps."

"Impossible," Iren said.

"We're the only ones standing between free humans," he indicated himself and Talia, "and the entire human race being converted into robot-controlled cyborgs."

Shit.

"There is one ray of hope. A scientist researching how to remove the stents has had a breakthrough."

"Great—"

"Unfortunately, she was researching on the prison planet. She has since disappeared. If she is still alive, it's possible she, and all her research, is Daz's next target."

No.

"We have to get to Daz first!"

"That's impossible," Sirus said, and softened it with his trademark optimism. "But, Daz could run into another person like you, Talia, who has the 'corruption gene.' Corruption, in this case, is corrupting robot controls."

Awesome. She hadn't lost the genetic lottery; she had won hands down. She was corrupting robots. "Can I hack into electronics?"

"Can you?"

"Not that I've ever noticed."

"Then no, probably not. But do let us know if your power extends itself."

Logen squeezed her. "You've corrupted me."

Well, that wasn't too bad either.

"What about contacting the rest of the mercenary corps?" Iren asked.

"Bad Company is on it."

Logen lifted a brow.

"Sure," Iren said, falling into the second's position almost naturally. "Because they did so much for us last time."

Yes, the Bad Company CO beat Logen.

But he had dropped the tractor, and gathered the intel, and had also outrun the initial assault on the planet in a weaponless shuttle, and then reconnected with his main ship and out-maneuvered the continuing assault, saving his unit and all the biologists from the fate suffered by the Misfits.

He was a different unit, but they were still part of the same corps.

Sirus paused, a half-smile on his face. "You know what our old motto used to be? *We all go home.* It doesn't matter what we have or don't have, who we're facing or our odds. We all go home."

She mouthed it silently. Next to her, she saw Logen's lips moving the same. It had been a long time since anyone had said it. She had missed Sirus.

"We're going to go to get Daz first," Sirus said. "Navina's home planet may already be collaborating with the Robotics Faction, so we're going to get her next."

"Wait. You let her pay out, because you're planning to convert her into a double-agent?" Iren asked. "Because I know you let Talia and Logen pay out, because you knew they were going to reenlist."

Sirus grinned and shrugged. To anyone who didn't know him, he looked so reckless. So careless, but at the same time, as Iren had pointed out, so insidiously clever.

"What about Vi?" Talia asked.

Maybe her tone was plaintive, or maybe she had imagined this final reunion differently. It was so hard to believe Vi had abandoned her. Abandoned all of them. Almost as hard to believe as Daz trying to kill her and Logen. Almost as hard to believe fourteen years ago, Sirus had abandoned them.

He hadn't abandoned them. He'd been fighting the Robotics Faction all of this time. She had to have more faith in her team. Perhaps Vi had a story as well.

Talia was willing to take it on faith.

Logen rubbed her back.

"We're going to get Vi," Sirus said.

"I think she's done with us," Iren said. "She didn't fight when she got converted. It was like she welcomed the stents."

"We're not done with her." A thread of steel firmed his tone. Declaring a campaign, willing them onto it despite fear, regret, opposition. They were up to it, his tone said. And they all straightened.

They were going to stop the Faction. They were going to free their soldiers from the mind control of the stents. They were going to reunite their team.

Sirus finished his beer and set it upside down on the stained table. "Any more objections?"

Iren considered it.

She and Logen finished their beers, the familiar yeasty promise uniting them in a shared past and a determined future. Iren followed their example, making a face at the bottom-barrel flavor, and also slamming it rim-side down. They all leaned in, a single team, four of them against the entire fucking universe. A CO, a Grunt, a Gun, and a Spot in the lowest pay level of the merc corps with the shittiest equipment, including an old fishing ship piloted by a half-crazed swashbuckler with the tractor bolted somewhere to the outside.

Talia snuggled into Logen's arms. She absolutely loved it, and from the tightening of his grip and Iren's more chipper determination, she knew they did too. Together, they would walk to the ends of the worlds to save their team.

"You've got another question," Sirus told Iren, reading him like a book.

"Yeah," he said. "When do we start?"

Sirus grinned. "Right now."

ABOUT THE AUTHOR

Wendy Lynn Clark is an award-winning author of contemporary and science fiction romance. She lives for delicious tea, her two cats, and hiking in the gorgeous Cascade mountain range. Find out more by visiting her online home at http://wendylynnclark.com.